MATRIMONIAL MERGER

CAL AND DAPHNE'S NEXT CHAPTER

LAKESHORE EMPIRE

MAUDE WINTERS

For the women who take back their stories even when it hurts.

AUTHOR'S NOTE

This is a continuation of Cal and Daphne's story, so it is not meant to be read as a standalone. Please catch up with their storyline first in *Executive Decision*.

CONTENT EXPECTATIONS

This book contains:

- Discussion of past abuse (including SA) but with no graphic description on the page.
- Discussion of past infertility and current pregnancy.
- Very spicy scenes and dirty talk.

PART I

THE TAKEOVER

PART I

THE TAKEOVER

1. KNACKERED

Daphne

"You look really tired," my brother Davey said, concerned. "Are you sure you're okay, Daph?"

"I'm good," I promised, covering a yawn.

"Let me bring you home—"

"No, I'm good. Are you okay with the presentation?"

"Got it," Davey closed his laptop. "I am a big boy. The spring campaign will be a hit. Promise."

I smiled, proud of myself. We had new brand partnerships rolling in. Licensing deals were my new favorite topic. And yet? I was having a hard time feeling joy today. I felt under the weather and exhausted. I should have been excited about announcing our new exclusive handbag deal. Instead, I wanted to crawl into bed and go to sleep.

My brother stopped by the door. "You sure you don't want a ride—"

"I'm going to Mum's," I said. "I need to pick up a dress and shoes from my closet there."

"Fundraiser?" Davey said.

"The mayor's fiancee needs to look beautiful." I rolled my

eyes. "So, here we go. Mum had the housekeeper steam a couple options."

"Well, good luck, First Lady of Chicago," Davey teased. "I'll see you bright and early tomorrow."

I gave him a playful salute and slipped my computer in my briefcase. Off I went to my family's home on North Astor Street. Cal, my fiancé, and I moved in together months ago—seemingly piece-by-piece. Both busy beyond recognition, we struggled with a focus on moving everything at once. Thus, most of my evening gowns still resided in my childhood closet.

When I arrived back home, I tossed my bag and shoes aside.

"Who is it?" Mum called from the formal living room. It was our housekeeper's day off.

I called out, "Daphne. I'm just here for a dress!"

My mother was busy with something else and thankfully just responded, "Ah, yes."

It left me alone to go upstairs and sort through the options on my own. I'd amassed a collection of dresses fit for a queen in the fall, always on display as Cal's girlfriend. But after our engagement was announced over Thanksgiving, my social calendar exploded more. This week, we had three Christmas parties to attend—thankfully only one was white-tie. In the new year, I was looking down the nose of multiple engagements a week of varying formality. Thankfully, when your family owned a high-end department store and you spent sixty hours a week there, you could grab whatever you wanted the minute it showed up. The personal stylists knew to call me when they got something good.

"It's Christmas. Go with the red."

I turned, seeing my mother in peripheral.

"I dunno. I thought black was fine."

"Oh, no, darling! Impossible! It's a party! What is it for?"

"This is for the Chicago Democrats," I said.

"Black is in poor taste. The Lanvin is much better."

"How did you—"

"I know everything," Mum said, satisfied. "I remember when you bought that. It's beautiful on you."

"I dunno." I shook my head and held out the body con gown. "I feel bloated."

"You'll look lovely in it. Wear it," Mum pleaded.

I tossed the Red Lanvin and black Dior down on the bed and stared at them.

"Are you feeling alright?" Mum asked, voice concerned.

"I'm fine," I said. "Why does everyone keep asking that? Davey was ready to bring me back to Cal's and tuck me into bed."

"Because you look knackered. Are you sure you don't need a nap."

I let out a long sigh. "Do I need a nap? Yes. Will I get one? No. I have two hours to look perfect. It's chaos."

Mum turned me, pulling my chin to hers. She rotated my face one way, then the other. As she examined me down to the pores, I pulled back. "Mum, I am *fine*."

"No, you're not. Are you sick?"

"I'm not. I felt off this morning, but recovered by noon. I didn't take anything. I think I'm just tired. I wanted to take a nap on my couch at lunch. I promise I will sleep better or something. It might be PMS?"

Mum grimaced. "PMS? You've never had PMS."

"Mother, I absolutely have! I just don't whine about it. I have terrible cramps—"

"But are you on your period?"

I shrugged, "I don't even know. Sometimes I don't get big periods anymore. The pill helps."

"And you've been taking them reliably?"

"Mostly," I answered.

Mum left, turning and dipping into the bathroom I shared with my younger sister, Dahlia, in a past life.

Mum emerged. "I will do your hair.. But first? I need you to do something."

"What?" I asked.

She handed me a pregnancy test. "Take this."

I rolled my eyes. "I've spent all of my thirties trying to get—"

"I will do your hair. Just take the test."

I groaned, lamenting. Holding the test in my hands, I cursed this fate. These things haunted me—always gleefully laughing in my face. I flashed back to a time when it was constantly a no. No matter what science said, my ex always felt it was my fault. As many times as I'd cried alone in a bathroom afraid to leave it, this felt loaded.

Looking at myself in the mirror, I said. "Fuck it. Let's just do this."

I closed my eyes, turned my chin towards the test, then bravely looked. What faced me first sent a shock down my spine. Then, I covered my mouth, dumbfounded. A moment before, I was certain I'd be reliving the pain and stress of many past trials, but standing there, it fell away. I picked up the test, pulling it closer in disbelief.

"I'm... pregnant," I whispered.

Saying it out loud finally made it real. But, as happy tears welled in my eyes, reality set in. This was good news—the news I'd wanted for more than five years—but it was also a bad time. We should have waited. I should have been better about my pills. And yet? I didn't hate it. I only worried about the damage it could do to Cal.

* * *

Cal

"Are you sure Daphne wants to spend the day packing bags for needy children?" Jo asked, eyebrow raised.

"Uh... sure," I said, typing.

"Cal!"

I pulled away from my focus on the screen at her tone. Jo

could scare me shitless with her righteous indignation. I needed it.

"Sorry, what?"

"I asked if you really meant to send Daphne out to pack bags —without you."

"Well, she's always a good sport," I said. "Just check with her assistant."

Jo's face didn't change. "If my husband voluntold me without asking for an all-day-long charity event, I'd lose it."

"She's the city's First Lady. It's what she does," I said. "She knows the job. Just clear it with her people. She loves kids."

"I will put it as tentative. Cal, she's not your goodwill envoy to deploy. She's the president of a retail holdings company. And while people may expect her to play the good wife, you have to be more mindful."

I was surprised for the pushback.

"Two months ago, you were saying if we were going to deploy her at all, we needed to soften her image. She ended up being great at charity—"

"There is a limit, sweetheart," Jo said.

I snickered. It had been *ages* since she'd given me such a dressing down. "Okay, I see your point. I just also see that she wants to be distracted. This year is going to be *hard* for her without David. It's the first Christmas—"

"Is it hard for her? Or you? Is it that *you* might be avoiding some of these things because it is also hard for you?"

Speechless, I sat there aghast at the assumption.

Jo took a deep breath. "Cal, I know you handle things differently. You get down in your feelings and stand around contemplating things—you can be brooding. Meanwhile, Daphne buries herself in work. But, you both need to talk about this. I am not going to be here for the crash."

I sighed. "You're not wrong, okay? I will... I will talk to Daph. Put it as tentative for now."

She nodded, standing and walking to the door.

"And Jo?" I asked.

She turned. "Yes?"

"Thanks for calling me on my bullshit."

"Anytime," she agreed.

I looked out the window. It wasn't the best view I'd had—not by a long shot. It didn't compare to the beautiful, expansive one I'd had at Delphine's. However, it was well-earned. The city was aglow, trying to make life festive. It was a beautiful time of year for Chicagoans. The windows in Delphine's blew everyone out of the water. The cultural center would glitter tonight for our annual Christmas gala. And yet? I wasn't feeling very jolly. I was missing my friend and helping my fiancée's family through a difficult season.

Jo poked her head back in. "You should leave, Cal. You still have to get ready. And while you can be a *little* late, you know your mother will—"

"Gotcha," I said. "I will finish up this email and hit the road."

No one wanted my mother's ire—much less Daphne. Things between them were still complicated. A merger of the Delphines and Markhams was perhaps predictable, but not preferable for Elise Markham—something ironic considering her retail partnership with Delphine's. We were still "new". Daphne's old-guard family had always annoyed her. And while Daphne only wanted there to be peace, Mom found any reason to complain. I heeded Jo's words and headed out.

2. LIFE HITS FAST

Daphne

THE BUZZ FROM DOWNSTAIRS CAUGHT ME OFF GUARD. I WAS IN our bedroom trying on my dress, cursing the bloat and my mother's insistence that I looked fine when I heard it. I crossed the room to answer it, annoyed that Cal was still on his way home. If this was who I thought it was, I dreaded what happened next.

"Hello?" I answered.

The concierge responded, "Miss Delphine, Mrs. Markham is here. She'd like to be let up."

"And I used to be!" I heard Elise protest.

Fuck!

"Let her up," I said, too tired to have much to say.

"Yes, ma'am," he agreed.

I went back to the bedroom to finish putting in my earrings. I wouldn't wait around for her. She'd come find me—demanding to know where her son was—soon enough.

"Calvin!" Her annoyance rang out. "Are you *decent?*"

"Cal isn't here," I responded, screwing in my second earring. "He's on his way."

"Are you... decent?"

I rolled my eyes. "Yes."

"You don't need to sound so annoyed."

I made eye contact with Elise in the mirror. "Well, if you had *announced* your arrival two weeks ago, you wouldn't have been surprised."

At thirty-five, I refused to hear my future mother-in-law complain about walking in on us in the kitchen. And I wasn't in the mood to talk to her about anything—let alone about this. It was a fuck around and situation, as Cal's sister Chloe would affectionately say. Or, rather, we fucked around and *she* found out.

"I didn't think—" She changed her tone. "I won't go there. However, I do doubt I will eat here anymore."

That's fine!

She retreated while I finished looking myself over. I may have felt bloated. I may have worried about the dress, but I didn't worry about how Cal would feel. I touched my earrings, looking for strength just to power through how lousy I felt so I could be happy. They were a gift from my father on my twenty-first birthday. My ex called them "guache" so I hadn't worn them much until he was out of my life. Cal, though, loved them on me. I knew he'd tell me I was the most beautiful woman on earth. Moreover, that adoration would be truly genuine.

"Fucking hell! I'm so sorry, baby!" I heard Cal's voice booming from the living room.

By the time he made it to the bedroom, he'd thrown off his jacket somewhere and was unbuttoning his shirt. "Traffic was—"

He stopped upon seeing his mother. "Well, traffic was awful. Sorry. I should have walked."

"That's a ridiculous idea," Elise said. "People would hassle you."

"They're constituents, not the unwashed masses, Mom."

She gave him a quick kiss on the cheek and a hug, intercepting Cal before he could so much as greet me. It was *so* typical. Instead of paying her much mind, however, he turned to me.

"Well, you look… gorgeous," Cal said. "Damn. Give me like ten minutes."

"It's going to take more than that, Cal. You need to shave," Elise said.

I glared at her. "It's fine. No one cares about the stubble."

We were now at a standoff. And rather than give her any satisfaction, I kissed Cal—long and slow. Her Boy Mom bullshit wasn't impressing me. I was all out of fucks two hours ago. Now, my fucks were in the negative and I was in a burn-it-all-down mood.

"Ten minutes. I swear," Cal said, looking past me.

He expected Elise to leave, but she was being her overbearing most.

"Mom, a moment?"

"Fine fine."

I watched her disappear and let out the biggest breath of relief I could, which wasn't much given that I could barely breathe in the internal corset within this damn dress. Did it look good? Judging by Cal's reaction, it probably did. I was my own worst critic.

"I'm serious," Cal said, closing the door. "You look… amazing. I'd take you back to the studs right now if I didn't have a mother who is painfully early and you didn't look so put together."

I smiled. "I would probably take you up on that offer and stay in if I knew this wasn't the big party with all the big people."

He kissed me slowly. "It is. But you look beautiful."

Cal disappeared into the closet, unusually disheveled for himself. "So, I wanted to send you to the Toys for Kids event to pack things. I have a meeting, but I just thought it might keep you busy and your Dad always volunteered. What do you think?"

"When is it?" I sighed.

"Well, it's on Tuesday morning. There will be media but it's casual."

I winced, debating my next move.

"I will be honest with you, Daphne," Cal said. "I'm… I'm not in a place where I can do that one. I'm struggling. David—"

I cut him off. "If it's in the morning, I just… I can't."

"I know Tuesday mornings are your quietest time. Sorry. I just assumed—"

"Mornings are hard for me," I said. "And… will be."

"That's okay. I will figure something out. I… I'm struggling more than I thought I would. I don't mean to avoid things, but I'm human, Daphne."

"I know I am too," I said, my eyes meeting his in the mirror as he buttoned his tux shit. "It's okay. Normally, I'd say sign me up, but… I'm not finding mornings easy."

"Oh? Is this your new assistant? Are they dropping the ball? It's okay to—"

"Cal, I'm pregnant." I ripped off the bandaid.

Judging by his reaction, I couldn't tell if this was for the best or the worst. What was done was done. There was not fixing it. I couldn't just be *not* pregnant. At least I didn't *want* to be not pregnant. And he'd have to get his head around it.

* * *

Cal

"I'm pregnant."

The words dropped like a bomb. I struggled to process if she was being honest or if this was a test. Was it a joke? No, Daphne wasn't much for jokes—or even surprises. She'd never joke about this. I took in her expression as she reacted and spun around.

"Pregnant? Like… really pregnant?"

"I mean, is there another type of pregnant," Daphne said. "I had old tests in my bathroom at Mum's. She forced me to take one and yeah… I'm pregnant."

"Oh… so you just found out?"

"Yeah. And then I had to sit through silence as she did my hair."

"She wasn't happy?" I winced.

"I wouldn't use that word, now. She was supportive, but… it's certainly not what she wanted. Or me, for that matter."

I cocked my head, placing my hands on her hips. "Really? I expected you'd be excited, Daph."

"I am. Well, I would be under any other circumstance. I love you, Cal. I want to have a baby with you.It's not that. We're not married. It's a scandal waiting to happen. Mum is super Catholic. This is her worst nightmare. She loves me and wants us to be happy, so she's holding her tongue. But if you think this is good from optics—"

I kissed her, cutting off her words. I took her face in my hands, unsure what to say.

"Cal, I'm being serious!" She pulled back. "This is—"

"Stop," I said. "I cannot hear you spiral into this negative place where you doubt yourself. For the thousandth time, I don't give a fuck about the optics. I love you."

"You can say that… but I've been a hot mess, Cal."

"Baby, I do not care." I kissed her forehead. "Daph, it will work out."

"I have a legal nightmare across the Atlantic. We have a wedding in June—a wedding where I will be embarrassingly pregnant. And the press will go bananas—"

"Well, Chandler's trial is one thing. I cannot fix that, but I will remind you that you are testifying for yourself and every woman who has ever experienced that level of betrayal."

"Revenge porn isn't a good look for you. Quarter three calmed the board down and all these brand deals are keeping them happy, but a surprise pregnancy and being out on leave? That's *after* the honeymoon, the wedding, the media hype? It will go over like a brick."

"The best part of this not being a publicly-traded company is that you can tell them to fuck off—"

"As long as they don't fire me."

"Well that would be a violation of federal, state, and municipal law, Daphne. Put on your lawyer hat for a moment. That will not happen. And Davey? He'd hand them their asses."

"He's going to be so angry with me."

I shook my head. "No. He will handle it. Give him a bit more credit."

Daphne raised her eyebrows. "Are you *defending* Davey? Has hell frozen over?"

"He stood by you when it mattered, okay? He's learning. And either way, he's terrified of your mother and she'd lose her shit over this. No. You're safe—there and here. Your priority should be your health, not optics or me or your family."

"But it is overwhelming and—"

"Cal!" Mom banged on the door. "We are going to be very late—"

My eyes never leaving Daphne's, I said, "It will still be there, Mom. I need a bit more time."

She left in a huff.

"She's driving me crazy and I'm over it," Daphne said. "The next thing she says to me cross-wise, I'm going to lose my shit."

"One moment," I said, walking to the door and poking my head out. "Mom, I have to deal with something. Take the car and go ahead. The driver can pick us up after he drops you."

"It will look bad—"

"It won't," I assured her. "But I need a minute to handle something. Can you just *please* go and meet Chloe there. We will follow shortly behind."

She crossed her arms, rolled her eyes, and relented. "Fine. But… you better not ignore it. I got all dressed up for *politics* and your god damn speech!"

"Yes, I am well-aware. And I will be there. Promise."

"I will go," Mom agreed.

I returned to Daphne, pulling the door closed. She looked at me tearfully and said, "Thank you. I just needed a minute."

"I know. I did, too."

"I'm sorry to spring this on you, but I cannot promise I won't be miserable and sick, Cal."

I gave her a long slow kiss, having to resit running my hands through her curls. Daphne's mother had piled her hair up atop her head and I didn't want to mess up all the good work.

"You shouldn't apologize. I love you, Daphne Delphine. I only wanted to soak you up a bit more. This is good news."

"It's a mess."

"It might be," I said. "Nothing about us is ever *simple*, alright? But it's wonderfully messy. You cannot be us and not have a little chaos, right?"

3. CHANGE OF PLANS

Daphne

CAL WOVE BEHIND ME, LOOKING OUT OVER THE ASSEMBLAGE OF people down below. The party went on, but I'd departed mentally ages ago. Between pretending to drink alcohol and playing the merry First Lady of Chicago, I was tapped out.

He whispered, "I want to take you home and do terrible things to you."

I turned, confused. "How much have you had to drink."

"This is water," Cal said, holding up a cup with a stir stick. "I've had two drinks. I am always on a leash."

"Why are you—"

"You're irresistible. I'm bored. I did my part—give the speech, am people up, look happy—but the only thing I really want is your ankles over my shoulders, princess."

I was tired, overstimulated, and socially drained, but his words threw me into overdrive.

He kissed me slowly, his hands resting too low on my hips. "C'mon. Let me unravel you."

I bit my lip. "Make an excuse and let's Irish goodbye this shit."

The last thing I wanted was Cal's famous, painful Midwest goodbye.

"Go down to the service entrance and I will meet you there."

Cal disappeared without a word and I obeyed his orders, feeling like I couldn't help myself. The idea of him going down on me was delicious. However, extricating him from a gathering was impossible. Everyone wanted to talk his ear off. We could never just *leave*. It was like my mother at a church luncheon—hopeless. I waited, preparing for disappointment. Instead, he appeared.

"I said you were exhausted, Jo was very sympathetic. She's going to be the bad guy," Cal said, taking my hand. "Let's go."

"Bless her," I said, relieved and surprised.

We piled into the car, partition raised. I thought we'd never make it off State Street, but we eventually did. In the elevator headed to our penthouse, Cal pinned me to the wall, kissing me like he needed me to breathe. It was a raw, hungry moment interrupted only momentarily by the elevator doors opening.

"Couch," I gasped. "I'm not going to make it to the bed."

"Oh, bad girl," Cal said. "She's *desperate*."

I fell to the couch. Cal pinned me, unable to resist. I pulled up the hem and skirt of my dress to free my hips a bit. Cal continued in that mission, running his hand up my dress.

"Do you *ever* wear panties, Daphne?" Cal asked.

"In this dress?" I gasped as he ran two fingers over my clit. I whimpered, "No."

"It's for the best," Cal said, kissing me again. As he did, he dipped his fingers inside me. It lit a fire within me and I ground against his hand.

I bit his lip and pulled back. "Are you not going to get to work, Mr. Mayor?"

"Yes, ma'am," Cal said.

To my surprise, he dropped to the floor and pulled me towards him. On his knees, he braced on the couch, burying his face in my pussy.

"Oh, fuck," I moaned, propping myself up on my elbows for the visual. "That is… so good."

He wasn't *always* so deferential, but damn I loved this. Cal was fully-absorbed in his desire for my pleasure. Laser-focused on my climax, he didn't stop until he'd met his objected. As his tongue did the work, his fingers kept time within me. I was about to squirt, so I stopped him.

"I… I'm gonna squirt," I panted. "You… we should probably…"

"What? You want me to stop, princess?"

"The couch—"

"Fuck the goddamn couch, Daphne. I want to hear you scream my name."

I gave over as he continued lapping me up—unbothered by what might happen to the couch.

"Oh, fuck," I moaned as his fingers found the best spot. "Yes, Cal! Right—"

I didn't finish my sentence, too far gone. My thighs twitched on his shoulders as I gave over to the earth shattering that followed. It took over my body. Tingles overcame me. It was like the best fireworks show, the sweetest ending.

"God, I love you," I panted as his eyes met mine again.

"Yeah? You like that?"

"It was so fucking good, baby," I moaned.

"Good, get on your hands and knees."

In the reflection of the windows, looking out over the skyline, I watched Cal take me from behind—both of us still *mostly* dressed. It was impatient, desperate fucking. But I loved the way he loved me—even as he lusted for me.

"God, you feel so fucking good, Daphne," Cal gasped. "I wanted you all night."

"Why?" I moaned.

"Because thinking impure thoughts about you while I talk politics is my favorite hobby. Especially when you look good enough to eat."

"And did you get what you wanted?"

"You were more than a snack," Cal answered, speeding up. He reached the most precious spot again—sending me far over the edge.

"Oh, fuck me, Cal! Fuck me!" I moaned. "Fuck me!"

"Are you summing for me, princess?" Cal demanded.

"Yes, baby, ye—" I screamed, unable to fight the feeling overwhelming me once more. I fell forward, hanging over the arm of the sofa, out of breath in the best way.

"Good girl, Daphne. Very good girl," Cal said.

It brought him over the edge, too. With one last thrust and a low, "Oh, fuck," he reached his own climax.

Hands digging into my hips, he panted and came down.

I looked back, a grin spreading on my face.

He mirrored my expression, spanking my ass. "You are a trip, Miss Delphine."

* * *

Cal

Daphne slept through my morning wakeup. I headed to the gym for a morning tennis lesson while she dozed. I hoped this morning would be an easier one for her. I didn't want to leave my warm, comfortable bed, but I had a long day ahead of me—an important one—and there was no rest for the wicked.

By the time I made it to the office, I was on my second cup of coffee, desperately trying to tell myself I was awake.

"Oh good, you're dressed down," Jo said, stopping in with the morning schedule. "Ready to pack gift bags?"

"Yes," I said. "I am."

"You don't sound like it. What was the sudden change of heart?"

"Well, I don't really have a choice. Daphne was busy."

"Uh-huh. How is she?"

Jo didn't buy my "Daphne is tired" excuse from the other night. She'd let it go until this moment. I had no time or energy and needed to cop to it, even if I didn't want to.

"Pull the door closed, if you would," I gestured. "Sit awhile."

"Oh no," Jo said, closing the door. "Trouble in paradise. Cal, I told you—"

"No, no!" I shook my head. "We're fine. There is no trouble in paradise. In fact, it's the absolute opposite. Daphne truly is tired and she's not well. The time I had you hold at four was actually for a doctor's appointment."

"Why? Oh, God! Is it cancer?"

My heart nearly stopped at the mere mention. "No, definitely not. Fuck cancer, but no. She's in good health. It's—"

"Cal, did you… you didn't. Did you?"

I winced.

Jo stood up, hand talking without words.

"Well, I don't know more right now," I said. "But hopefully I will later."

"Were you two not aware of your current status? That there is a wedding planned for *June*?"

"I know," I agreed. "But Daphne is… well, it's about the journey, right?"

"Cal, the journey and you making me pull my hair out! Can we ever just make things *easy*?"

"If they were easy, Jo, you'd be miserable."

She crossed her arms. "Well, congratulations. We are fucked, but you seem happy. And Daphne?"

"She's got terrible morning sickness and naps twice a day, but she's excited. We both want this… even if the timing is shit."

Jo shook my head. "Slow down."

"Impossible. I'm not getting younger."

"Take care of her. The entire city is going to go insane."

"Well, we will see what the doctor says," I said. "Daphne doesn't want to people to know yet. But I needed to let you know what was going on for obvious reasons."

"I am glad to hear it, no matter how much it fucks with your schedule. I will make sure to clear your August."

"What?" I asked.

"Cal, if she's having a baby in August—as I assume she is based on what you're telling me—then you won't be in, right?"

I hadn't thought about it. "I guess that is true?"

"Get on board, buddy. You're about to be a dad."

"It's fucking wild, isn't it?" I chuckled.

Jo sighed, "It was always going to happen. You love kids. It would be a true waste if it didn't. Tell Daphne congrats from me."

4. IT'S SOMETHING

Daphne

I smiled at the ultrasound on the top of my dresser in the bedroom. Every morning that I felt sick and miserable, I reminded myself good things were coming. Today would be hard—a very difficult day—but I'd use it to distract myself from the void left by loss. Dad wasn't here on this Christmas Eve, but he was always in our hearts. And today we threw ourselves into service as a family.

"Are you okay? You really shouldn't push it," Cal said, wrapping his arms around me and kissing my neck.

"I'm fine. I'm not made of glass, baby. This is important."

"I'm just fussing. Sorry. I worry about you."

I faced him. "I love you for that. But it's okay. This matters to me."

Cal kissed me, making me feel more at ease with this difficult day. His touch reminded me that we were both grieving. I could tell him how hard it was. I could love him.

"Can we just… walk over there?" I asked. "It's early and quiet, but I could use the cold air."

Cal kissed my forehead. "Of course, baby."

And that was that. Regardless of what the security people thought, we took a walk over to the service entrance of the store, ducking into the maze of hallways and back sets of stairs that led to my sister's kitchen. Today, we were assembling huge number of meals for hungry families rather than sitting around at home. We'd closed the restaurant in an act of community service. Volunteers—most of which were somehow related to the family—assembled around a table holding coffee.

Dahlia was the executive chef of the Dolphin Room, our newly-revitalized flagship restaurant. She was building out the foodhall downstairs, but for now the restaurant was her primary focus. Dahlia trained in Europe, worked in Paris, and like me, returned to Chicago to keep Dad's memory alive in her own way. This was her gift.

As we arrived, I realized the entire family was there—and then some.

I spotted Cal's stepfather, Tim, and his sister, Chloe, and quickly greeted them.

"What are you all doing here?" I asked.

"Well, Cal said we could come," Chloe said, giving me a tight hug that made my breasts scream for dear life.

I fought a grimace. "That's sweet of you."

"Even Mom came out," Chloe said, sounding genuinely surprised.

I grew concerned but beat that down. It was a nice thing to do. "Thanks for this. It would mean so much to Dad."

Mum rushed past me, holding a platter of biscuits and pastries. She said nothing, totally focused on her job. We'd never been close when I was younger. Mum hadn't been perfect—no parent was—but after Dad's death, we bonded unexpectedly. I began to realize that Mum was more like me than she wasn't. By digging in with both hands today, she was trying to cope with Dad's memory. Last year, we'd started mourning the life we thought we would have. This year, we came to terms with our new reality—Dad's booming laugh was nowhere to be heard. His warm smile wasn't seen. His great big hugs were no more.

Instead, as I looked around the room, I listened to my little brother Derrick's laugh—so much like Dad's. I saw my baby sister Dora helping mom lay out the snacks for volunteers. She was so generous. She had Dad's heart. Delanie, came up to laugh with Chloe, who was her best friend. The two hugged, knowing the day was as hard as it was special. Davey helped Dahlia with setup. He had the weight of the world on his shoulders now.

Cal wrapped his hand around my waist as I fought tears.

"Are you doing okay?" He asked.

"I'm about to be a crying mess," I said. "I don't even know why."

"I could think of reasons," Cal said sweetly.

"It's okay. We're doing the best we can. We're fine. Fine will be enough for the day, right?"

Cal kissed the top of my head. "Fine is more than enough for this season."

* * *

Cal

By noon, I could tell Daphne flagging. Everything I'd read about pregnancy suggested that it was hard on a woman's body. I wondered when her go-go-go attitude would return. She was so dedicated that her reticence to carry on signaled she really *did* need a break. I walked up to the table where she was putting rolls into carryout containers, a job she chose because it was the least smelly option and required no heavy lifting.

"Why don't you take a break," I suggested.

No fight left, Daphne said, "I'm so tired."

"Get some water and sit," I said.

She nodded weakly. I stepped in, taking a break from helping load the vans. I watched her take a seat by the catering table, digging into the plate of digestive biscuits. Satisfied that she was sitting down and *not* about to fall asleep like a horse in a stall, I turned back to what I was doing.

That was until my mother came towards me. "Why is Daphne sitting there?"

"She needed a break," I answered. "I decided to step in."

My mother let out a long sigh, then walked off. No matter what Daphne did or didn't do—no matter how perfectly—it would never be enough for Mom. It set me off. I stewed for a minute before turning to see Mom talking with Daphne. Or, rather, talking *at* Daphne. Seeing red, I strode over, hearing only a bit of their conversation. Daphne's give-a-damn was busted and her jaw was set. It was *not* looking good.

"Well, just drink some coffee. It will be alright," Mom said.

She would if she could, Mom!

"I'm fine," Daphne said. "I just need a moment."

"Mom, why don't you leave Daphne alone to rest?" I asked.

"We are *all* working. She's younger and healthier than you—"

"Mom," I said, tone sharp. "Leave her be. She's just taking a minute."

"Is there an issue?"

I turned to see Danna Delphine to my right and knew things had gone off the rails completely. There was about to be a battle among the city's proudest matriarchs. New clashed with old out of the gate.

"Daphne is taking a minute," I said.

"I am worried about her," Mom insisted. "She looks so pale. I told her to drink some coffee and she will feel better but she's refusing that."

"I'm good. Really," Daphne protested.

"And I told you, Mom, she's fine," I said. "Just a little over-whelmed."

Danna crossed her arms. "See, she's fine."

Mom, annoyed, rolled her eyes and left. Daphne looked up at

me, small as could be. All I wanted to do was hold her, but that was completely off the table.

"Elise, what is your issue? Did you come here to help or judge my daughter?" Danna called after her. "Because to my knowledge, Cal invited you out of the goodness of his heart but all you've done is chide us and make it about you."

Mum spun around. "Oh, like the hospital benefit you made *all* about you after my grandmother died? Where you put me on the worst committee?"

"Because you claimed to be too upset—"

"I was not too upset. You told me that I was too tacky to plan anything!"

"I never said such a thing!" Danna scoffed.

"No, you told Janine that, though!"

Danna set her jaw the same way Daphne had moments before. I knew it was about to come pouring out. Davey caught my eye, moving into view. I met his gaze, worried we might have to step in if hands were thrown.

"Regardless of what *I* did or did not do—"

"You did do it, though, Danna ! You did."

Danna repeated, "Regardless of what I did or did not do, my daughter has been nothing but gracious to you. She loves Cal. She is good to him. Is that not enough?"

"The way he treats her like some wounded bird annoys the hell out of me!" Mom declared, throwing her arms around. By now, Tim emerged from the background.

"This is not the time, Elise," Tim said.

"It probably isn't, but I don't give a damn, Timothy! Danna has poked the bear! Every time there is even something the least bit wrong, Cal swoops in to save Daphne and it's a whole thing. Cal has been swooping in to save you all for years—at his own disservice many times."

"Mom, I am a grown man. And Daphne is no damsel."

"Well, she shouldn't be. She's an educated heiress who is insisting on a lock tight prenup, correct? She knows the game."

"Game?" Danna asked. "What game?"

"She bats her eyelashes and he comes running. It was the same thing with you and David. God forbid David need something, Cal would be—"

"David was my best friend!" I said, unable to hold back. "He was my mentor and one of the best men I ever met. I owe him a great deal of credit. And Daphne? Of *course* I rush in to take care of her. She's about to be my wife. If I didn't run to her, what sort of man would I be, mother?"

"Well, for a woman with all of her capabilities, I'd expect her to want to save herself!"

"Asking people for help is not a crime, mother," I said. "She said she needed to take a seat. In fact, I asked her if she was okay."

"And now you bloody well storm over here to interrogate her!"

"If she would just drink a cup of coffee—"

"But she can't!" Danna said protectively. I knew what came next and I braced for impact. "She is pregnant and cannot have coffee. And if you were not being an absolute cunt, you would leave it be!"

It was worse than expected, to the point that Danna immediately recoiled and covered her mouth. She knew she shouldn't have said the first bit and the second bit, though absolutely true, wasn't helpful. But, given that the woman was a widow and wildly protective of her brood of six children, I gave her a pass. This was a hard day for everyone.

Daphne stood, tears in her eyes. "Can we all just shut the fuck up and let me cry in peace?" She stormed past me and I tried to follow her but she pushed me away and said, "No! I do not need you involving yourself, Cal!"

It hurt. I knew she wasn't mad at me, just very overwhelmed. And, anyhow, I had issues to deal with on her behalf. The room was quiet enough to hear a pin drop—and enough to hear Daphne sobbing in the back of the kitchen.

"She's pregnant?" Mom demanded. "And I'm finding out—"

"Elise, drop it!" Tim said, voice strong. Tim rarely raised his voice, but when he did, Mom listened.

"God damn it! What is going on! Why is Daphne sobbing next to the cooler?" Dahlia's voice rang out as she strode over. "What the actual fuck?"

"Ask Elise," Danna said.

"Excuse me, but you just called me a cunt!"

"What now?" Dahlia did a double-take, glaring at Danna .

"My words were regrettable," Elise said.

"And, mother?" Davey said.

"I apologize for using that word."

"And are you going to apologize to Cal and Daphne or just Elise?" Delanie asked. "Because you just told everyone Daphne's very private news pretty openly!"

Tears welled and Danna collapsed into a chair, sobbing openly. I'd never seen the woman cry—not even at David's funeral—so this shook me.

Delanie threw her hands in the air.

"It's okay. Tensions are running high," I said. "I'm not angry."

Dahlia stood on a chair and clapped her hands. "Okay! Everyone! The goal here is not to kill one another! Everyone is sad. Dad isn't here. And lord knows if he were here, he'd have just lost his mind upon hearing that he was about to—"

Dahlia fought tears as well. "About to… get his first grand-child and… oh fuck!"

She got down, now completely sobbing. The entire room was about to cry. I could feel it.

Davey shouted, "This is about Dad. It's about his spirit and wanting to take care of everyone. As lovely as this news is, can we please stop fighting and focus on why we are here and the good we are doing?"

"We're here to take care of our neighbors," I agreed. "So, let us focus on that. And then those of you who can drink and need a drink later will get their chance. Right now, though, we still have work to do. Let's do that much for David's memory, alright?"

"Okay, everyone," Dahlia said. "We have two more hours here to pull this together. Can we please get back to work—everyone but Cal and Daphne. They get a pass."

I shot her a smile and went to find Daphne.

5. KNOCKED UP

Cal

"Mom, can I pull you out for a minute to chat?" I asked.

Mom's face dropped. She turned from where she was speaking with Tim and said, "There is nothing to say. I regret—"

"There are things to say—things *I* need to say. Follow me," I said.

She relented, following me through the back entrance to the kitchen, then down to the ground floor and out a back door that connected the store to the company's tower. With Daphne's keycard, I had access to everything. We took the executive elevator up, nostalgia hitting immediately. Mom said nothing. She was on-edge—aware she'd fucked up, but also not sure how to fix it.

I walked down the hallway past the assistants in the center of the c-suite area. I nodded and said, "Just using Daphne's office."

They nodded back, not batting an eyelash.

We ducked into Daphne's office. Mom popped down on the sofa in the corner, seething, while I tried to find the words to tell her how hurt I was.

"Does it have you all nostalgic?" Mom asked. "Or did you just bring me to humiliate me?"

I chose my words carefully, looking out the plate glass wall, across to David's old office. I expected to see the company's late patriarch popping in. Now, it was changed, full of Davey's sports memorabilia these days. The view remained the same, but much had changed. I thought about my old office up the hall. I thought about everything I'd learned and felt here. It was overwhelming —like a ghost town left behind.

I leaned on Daphne's desk, "I brought you here because it's the busiest shopping day of the year, Mom, and I wasn't about to lay into you in front of a crowd. Nor can I let you and Daphne share oxygen right now without worrying about what will happen to her."

"I am not going to hurt her, Calvin. It was Danna—"

"Let's leave Danna out of this," I said. "She's a grieving widow. This entire family is grieving—and that includes me, Mom. Have a heart."

She looked down at her hands, folded in her lap. "In retrospect, I should have let up on the girl."

I rubbed my temples. "Mom, she's not a girl. She's a woman. And I wish you would treat her like she is an equal. She's a business woman, just like you. Why can you not just let it go? What is your beef with Daphne?"

"She's nothing like me! Or you! All of these people are robber barons. This entire place was just *handed* to them. They've always had it easy. Always! They aren't like you, Cal. And you? You deserve someone who understands that. Daphne is lucky she was born into wealth and always had an easy time of it."

I approached, sitting on the couch across from her. "Mom, she was born into privilege but you don't get to choose your parents. Why would you take it out on Daphne?"

"Because it is people like Daphne—and Danna before her— that have always spat and me and all I did."

"Mom, Delphine's has given you a *killer* brand deal. Your stuff ended up on the faces of the richest women in this town in Q4. Daphne did that. Chloe and Daphne together, in fact. Would you like me to bring you to Chloe's office and show you what the Chief Influencer's office looks like?" I asked. "Because Daphne did that. And if you're into eating the rich, just remember that Chloe has never wanted for anything in *her* life. Is she less capable? I'd hate anyone to describe her that way—to infantilize her or suggest she was less-than—and I'm pretty sure you agree."

Mom shook her head, gaze dropping. "Calvin, you do not understand anything about these people."

"I have lived my entire life trying, so I think I know *a bit*."

"Do you? Because you deserve this—all you've worked for—and you have the satisfaction of it."

I cocked my head. "What do you mean?"

Mom stood, walking to the bookcase behind Daphne's desk.

"You struggled with me. I gave you *everything* I could. I dedicated my life to making it out—for you—and you made it out. But you ended up in bed with people who don't understand any of that. And now? Now I have to share grandchildren with that... that woman?"

"That woman is Daphne's mother. And she just lost her husband and is suffering through the holidays without him—we all are."

"Yeah, well no one gave a shit about the fact that your father ran off and then took his own life a year later in Florida," Mom said. "No one cares about me and what I went through as a teenage mother—the type of person everyone loathes and judges. *That* is why Daphne's mother went off on me."

"It's not," I chuckled. "It's really not."

Mom rolled her eyes. "This is what I am talking about—"

"Mother, she doesn't think about you. Danna doesn't give a flying fuck about you. You two may sometimes share air, but you're right... you have little in common."

"I have beat her in *numerous* tennis competitions—"

"It doesn't matter. She has her friends. Those friends are... never going to be your friends. And I won't ever understand it.

Nor will Daphne, who isn't like her mother in oh-so-many-ways, Mom. Daphne isn't pretentious. You'd know that if you ever sat down and had a conversation with her that wasn't a series of questions in a deposition."

"Daphne's mother—"

"Went off on you because Daphne was feeling ill and she knew Daphne was pregnant. The only people who did were Danna, Jo, and myself. You set her off. Just like you go off when you think one of us is being sidelined, Danna went off to defend her daughter. And I get the impulse because you are testing every bit of my patience right now. Daphne is upset. She's done. She was done with you before she even knew you were going to be here."

"Why?"

"You've never said a god damn nice thing about Daphne!"

"I said she was well-educated."

"Only to imply that she's privileged as hell."

"All she does is argue—"

"She's an attorney."

"Doesn't that get old?"

I smiled. "No. I love her. I couldn't want anyone else if I tried, Mom. She's fucking perfect. I'm as happy as I have ever been."

Mom's face dropped like I'd just kicked a puppy.

"Mom, I think you think she should have suffered more to deserve the success she got, right?"

She didn't respond.

"That's ludicrous. And it's insulting. In two weeks, she's getting on a plane to go testify in court about a man sending revenge porn tape to other cabinet ministers before leaking it to the media—"

"And yet, that doesn't bother you? That she—"

"Stop it! The next words out of your mouth should be anything but a suggestion that she's unworthy because someone abused her—the way my sperm donor did me before leaving."

Mom's gaze dropped again.

"I didn't love struggling," I said. "I didn't love being the man of the house always. I didn't enjoy being an outsider who constantly felt the need to prove I fit in—that I was *one* of them. I'm not. I never will be. That's fine. I didn't want to be. But to think everyone should have to suffer and struggle? I am fighting every fucking day to make things *less* of a struggle for people, Mom. Childhood trauma isn't a god damn badge of honor."

"It makes you a better person to come from something—to work."

"And Daphne has. She has worked."

"You had to struggle. You can call it trauma—call it what you like—but it made you the man you are today, Cal," Mom insisted.

I stood and shook my head. "No, Mom. You did. David did. Life did. I worked my ass off—just like I watched you do. But it wasn't without problems. It wasn't without issues. You think Chloe and I are perfect for some ungodly reason—"

"Because you are both wonderful."

"And that's sweet. You're supposed to say that. You're our mother. But, mom, I'm forty-eight, unmarried, and have a job that demands my attention night and day. I am sometimes emotionally unavailable and exhausted. A normal woman— someone you'd probably prefer—wouldn't put up with me. Daphne? She is made of similar stuff, okay? Leave her be. Or, so help me, you will have *no* access to our child. Because for the life of me, I cannot imagine why anyone who cannot love their mother for all she is needs to be in their life."

Tears welled in my mother's eyes. "Cal, don't say—"

"Mother, you have a choice. Back off of Daphne or deal with my silence," I said.

"But Danna—"

"Ignore Danna! You don't have to ever say a god damn word to Danna. I know things aren't roses between you. I am not asking you to be best friends with Danna—even Daphne. But Daphne? She's going to be my wife. She's the mother of my child. So, you're going to play nice and be nice to her or so help me, you won't be in the picture at all."

"That isn't fair—"

"It is. It's not fair to Tim, perhaps because Tim hasn't done anything but welcome Daphne."

"I will… try. But we have little in common."

I groaned. "Mother, what do you mean? Other than a massive brand deal with her company? Yeah, you're lucky that Daphne's business acumen outweighs her revenge complex."

* * *

Daphne

"Daph, are you feeling any better?"

"I just want to rest," I groaned, looking up at Cal.

I lay on the couch in my late father's study—the room no one dared touch. Cal stood over me, face sympathetic. He sat a mug down on the coffee table. "Hot cocoa—with extra marshmallows, per Dora."

"Thanks," I said, sitting. A warm beverage and chocolate sounded good. And—unlike the coffee I craved deep in my bones—this was technically safe to drink.

Cal sat next to me, unfurling his arm across the back of the couch.

"I don't know what to say," he said. "Other than I am profusely sorry that my mother acted like a monster. I feel so shitty, Daph."

I rested my head on his shoulder. "I don't blame you. She's fucking mad, but… maybe I don't quite understand it yet? Maybe motherhood makes you lose your fucking mind for no reason?"

He wrapped his arm around me. "I think that is probably what set your mother off, but it's no excuse."

"An explanation?"

"Maybe. I'm sorry. It's be a hard day."

"Oh, it's all my fault."

"How?" Cal asked. "Baby, you didn't do anything other than exist. It's not like anyone let you get a word in."

"No, they didn't. And that's why I just left," I said. "But… if I wasn't pregnant, everything wouldn't be melting down around me. I'm so tired. I have no fight left. I just want to take a nap for two months and wake up when the nausea is gone."

"It will improve. And things won't always feel this heavy."

I met his gaze. "Really, Cal? Because all I hear is that I am going to be forced to be the knocked up bride who is embarrassingly big on her wedding day—like a walking embarrassment. If all of this—if having to go on record about the fact that yes, that was me naked in that video—wasn't bad enough, let alone being the shameful unwed pregnant woman."

"Daph, you're going to be beautiful—"

"I don't want that, Cal. I ran away from my first wedding and was brought back kicking and screaming. Now? Now I have to do it seven months pregnant! It's mortifying!"

"You don't need to be embarrassed. This isn't the sixteen hundreds, baby."

"Well, it's not just that. I also…" I couldn't say the words.

"What?" Cal shifted his weight, looking at me head-on.

"I just.. I'm going to have go down the aisle alone—without Dad—and… it sucks." Tears welled in my eyes for the thousandth time that day. "I will be embarrassed *and* sad. At least the first time, I had him there with me. It was the only good part of that day. And I should have savored it all more."

"Oh, my love," Cal sighed. "I'm sorry."

He held me tight as I cried, finally admitting the thing that bothered me most about any sort of wedding planning. I couldn't imagine standing at the beginning of a church aisle alone without my father.

"It's why I've drug my feet on planning," I sniffled. "Because as stupid as it sounds, I cannot visualize it without crying. It feels so lonely and hard. If he were here, he'd be... so happy. And now... he'd want to meet this baby. It's all he ever wanted—to be a grandfather. But I just... I cannot stomach planning it. I want to marry you. I want that so much, Cal. But the wedding? It all feels so sad and pointless. Because even the things I was excited about—picking a dress that *I* loved, rather than what I thought everyone wanted and having a beautiful spring wedding with all of our families—it feels ridiculous now. All I think about is how I'm going to overheat in June and sob the entire way to you. And how I will hate our pictures and regret all of that—not the marriage, just the wedding. And I'm shallow and I care—"

He handed me a tissue. "You're not shallow, Daphne. Not at all. You're allowed to want to look at your pictures and not hate them. And you're allowed to miss David. You're allowed to wish he was alive. I know I did today—a lot."

"Really?"

"Of course. Daphne, I was sitting in your office expecting to see him any minute. Of course, I'd hear his laugh before I'd see him with any luck."

I smiled before descending into tears again. "Oh, fuck, I know just what you mean. And I just miss him so much, Cal."

"We could get married sooner—"

"Cal, our engagement party isn't even until February. And your mother—"

"I don't give a flying fuck what our mothers do or don't want. Yours had her way the first time. She is aware this isn't about her. Mine? She can fuck right off. I told her if she cannot treat you with respect, she doesn't get to be in our lives—and that includes the baby."

"You what?" I gasped.

"I told her she could either behave or she'd not know our kid. Daphne, being a grandparent is a fucking privilege. The last thing I want is for our baby to grow up thinking it is okay for another adult to treat their mother like dogshit."

"To be fair, my mother is no angel and--"

"She called my mother a cunt? I am aware. But… she deserved it."

I snickered. "Jesus Christ. I never thought she'd utter such a thing."

"Her baby was sick and Mom kept poking at you on a day where everyone was having a breakdown without David. I get it. I saw red. I think she will behave—I hope she will. And it doesn't matter. We will do what we want to do. What do *you* want to do? Do you want to wait until after the baby is born? We could have a long engagement, I guess?"

I could tell the suggestion pained Cal. He'd have married me tomorrow if I asked him.

"I don't want to wait until I'm nursing a new baby and trying to figure my shit out," I said. "No. We'll only be *more* exhausted. I wouldn't want to wait."

Relief spread across his face.

"I love that you want to marry me so much you were willing to wait even *longer*," I giggled. "But that's not what I want. I think the only thing worse than being a very pregnant bride is trying to explain for another year that I'm just the mayor's girlfriend for another year."

He kissed my forehead. "You are never *just* anything, Daphne Delphine. You're everything. I would marry you anywhere, anytime if you'd let me."

I smiled. "I feel the same. But I do actually want to have *some* sort of wedding. I will be okay. I'm just mourning what I thought the day would be. It doesn't look anything like I thought it would, but it doesn't matter. I'm marrying the person I love. And I'm finally having a baby. I should be happy."

"You will," Cal said. "And if you're worried about walking down alone, don't. I think your brothers would be happy to help. It will look different, but the world is different than the first time I kissed you in that conference room. And maybe that's not for the worst?"

I held his face in my hands. "Cal Markham, you're everything

I could ever want, but you're right. Both of us lived, learned, and had to get here."

"Sorry it took so many twists and turns," Cal said.

I leaned in, kissing him slowly. He was the only one I needed right now—the only one I cared to entertain, too. I was safe here.

"The best deals are rarely linear," I said. "M & A takes time, baby."

He snickered. "Only you would mention M&A during wedding planning, Daphne."

"It is technically a merger, is it not? Because I swear if you call this an acquisition—"

Cal shook his head. "It never would be. This is far from a hostile takeover, princess."

PART II

THE PLAN

6. ONE LAST GLANCE

Daphne

I WAS PERCHED OVER MY DESK SIDE TRASH CAN WHEN I HEARD THE
sound of my brother's voice.

"Daph? You in here?"

He couldn't see me from where he was. I was physically *below*
the desk. I hoped maybe he'd leave me to this indignity and go
elsewhere, but Davey was as perceptive as a brick. So, he called
out once more, "Daph, if you're hiding—"

I raised my left hand and waved it, choking out, "I'm not
feeling well, but I'm here."

Davey rushed over, concerned, then backed away realizing
what was going on. I expected him to run—even gag—but he
just ran into the bathroom and returned with a cool, wet hand
towel.

"In case you like… need it," Davey said.

I slowly sat back up in my chair and put it on my forehead.
"I'm sorry. What do you need?"

His eyes remained on the trash.

"It's just a bin."

"With… puke…"

"I didn't puke. I dry heaved. I *thought* I would puke."

"That sounds awful."

"It is," I said, tired of talking about it. "What do you need?"

Davey sat on the edge of my desk. "Are you going to do the Chicago Business Week luncheon? They need a response and have been relentlessly bothering Melinda. And Anna says she knows nothing."

I groaned. "Because I never responded to your email. Must I? No one wants to see me. Can't you do it?"

"Daph, they *asked* for you. You are supposed to be their fucking keynote."

"I doubt they will care if you do it."

"The never have a woman keynote. The quarterly luncheon is always a dude. If they are asking for you, they want you. It's a sausage fest. You'd know if you ever went, sister."

I rolled my eyes. "Yes, another *very* inclusive space."

"Look, I am not going to claim it is. However, they want *you* and I think you should go."

I was drowning. I wanted so badly to say no.

Davey's face softened. "Daph, I know it's a lot. It's *so* much. You just survived the holidays. You're pregnant. You feel like shit. And tomorrow, you'll have to face something worse. I am here to support you no matter what, but the Daphne I know would want me to tell her to do it because she'll regret it if she doesn't."

His tone was earnest beyond measure, sweet even! Normally, all Davey did was become immediately frustrated and bark at me when he got whipped up.

"Are you getting soft, David?" I joked.

"No. I just... I care about you. And I care about company interests. The board would like to see you take a more visible role. I know that's not your bag. You aren't the schmoozer—"

"That is firmly you and Chloe."

"I know. And we're good at it, but this isn't our story to tell. And I'm not about to claim credit for your ideas to turn retail around in just a bit over a quarter. I worry about Dad coming back from the dead to curse me."

I snickered. "Okay. Fine. I will tell Anna I'll do the damn thing."

Davey smiled and stood again. "You're going to be glad you said yes. Promise."

A knock at the door made us both turn. Cal stood in the doorway. "Sorry. I didn't mean to barge in but you were on the way, Daph."

"You can't quit us, can you?" Davey joked.

"We have an appointment," I said. "He's just trying to force me to take the car rather than walk. I am fine, Cal."

"You're definitely not. She was just dry heaving into the trash five minutes ago!" Davey outed me. "What is that?"

Davey pointed to the can in Cal's hand. Cal raised it and answered, "Pomegranate seltzer."

"A bit early for that, bud, isn't it?" Davey joked.

"Davey, it's for me," I grumbled. "It settles my stomach. It's just flavored water, not White Claw."

"Oh," Davey said, facepalming. "Apologies. Well, good luck with whatever this is. Wedding stuff?"

"We're getting a scan," I answered. "And having a follow-up. For the baby. No wedding stuff."

"Don't mention it," Cal whispered. "It only makes things worse."

Davey patted Cal on the shoulder and left, calling back, "Good luck!"

I locked my computer and grabbed my purse. "I'm ready."

And nervous.

He gave me a quick kiss on the forehead before opening the door. "It will all be fine, baby. Promise."

"I love you."

* * *

Cal

The heartbeat rang out clear as a bell—strong and fast. I felt everything at once—excitement, nerves, pride. Daphne cried. I fought tears, maintaining composure by a hair—and ONLY a hair. Any worries dissipated like a puff of smoke in the wind as I held the second ultrasound in my hands. I thought parenthood would always evade me, but here I was looking at visual proof it was happening.

I listened in disbelief as the doctor outlined our next appointment—another scan to measure something and the genetic testing that would tell us if things were progressing and the baby was fine.

"Do we want to know the sex?" Daphne asked me.

"I don't really care," I said, watching her face drop. "But if you do… it's your body, Daphne. I am alright either way."

Her smile bounced back. "I want to know."

"Then, let's find out," I agreed.

She beamed. God, I loved that smile. That *beautiful* smile. Even when she felt like garbage and had a million worries across an ocean, she had the best smile.

We were headed back out of the office when Daphne looked at me. "What are you staring like me for that?"

"Can I not just stare at you?" I laughed.

"Like that?" No."

"Daph, I just love you so much. I cannot look at you like anything else. Forgive me for wanting to appreciate you. You're about to go to London for however long. I want to just enjoy you."

She blushed bright red. "Stop it."

"What? Does that fluster you?"

"I don't know why you say such sweet things—"

"Because I love you—a lot. And I'm happy, alright? I'm so happy."

She squeezed my hand. "Me, too. I am happier than I have ever been."

I opened my mouth to tell her I felt the same, but instead heard a familiar voice.

"Oh my God, Cal and Daphne. How are you?"

We both turned to see Kristy approaching. *Was she pregnant?* I couldn't help but look and thing she was.

"We're good," I answered, not sure what to say. "And you?"

She cupped her stomach, "My back is killing me, but I'm good."

"You're pregnant?" Daphne asked. "Again?"

Kristy brimmed, "Yep. About twelve weeks. We aren't really telling anyone yet. Too much pressure."

"Oh my God, that's amazing!" Daphne lit up.

Kristy gave me a look, as if wondering if we had more to say. I left that up to Daphne. She didn't offer it up. I didn't pry. I let her lead. The critical people knew she was pregnant. That was enough. And while Daphne and Kristy got along, I wasn't about to wade into that mess.

"It's been ages," Kristy said. "We should have you over. So much to catch up on. And we've never celebrated your engagement."

"You're invited to the engagement party next month," I said. "No worries."

"Okay, but we should grab dinner! It's been wild and we could use a night out sans-kid. I know I could anyhow."

Daphne looked to me. "Well, I'd like to as well. I am sure Cal would love to catch up, but I'm off to London for a little bit."

"Oh, well, I guess I'll see you in February. Or maybe before? Aren't you hosting that sustainability summit, Cal?"

"Yes," I answered. "So, maybe I will see you before? I didn't think about that."

"Cool," Kristy said. "Well, I've got to get poked and prodded. See you later."

She left and I treaded on eggshells as the doors to the elevator closed.

"You are allowed to catch up with her," Daphne clarified. "I trust you. I know Kristy is a close friend, Cal."

I turned, confused. "Well, out of respect—"

"Cal, I trust you. You're with me, not Kristy. We've babysat her kid. Come on now! I didn't realize you thought that. Cal, I deal with men on a daily basis and I wouldn't think twice—"

"I trust you to take a business meeting without me. I just… we have a history."

"She's your friend—one of your best friends."

I was astonished. "But Chandler—"

"Was a cheating asshole. He isn't you, Cal. I trust you. You are one of the few men I have ever felt completely safe with. So, catch up. Kristy is in a relationship. If her partner isn't worried, why would I be? And you can tell her. I trust her, Cal. I'd catch up *with* you, but I am about to be underwater and media scrutiny. You might need a break to complain after the press jump on you, too."

We reached the parking garage where my security waited with the driver.

"Daph, I don't care. They can come for me as much as they want. I am enraged for you and wish you would have let me—"

"Cal, you couldn't come," Daphne insisted. "And I don't want you there. I don't want you to have to sit through that conversation in real time. It will be harder for me to say those things in front of you."

I climbed into the car after her, confused about why she was reticent.

"I already know them, Daphne."

"I know. But… it's so much harder to know you are reliving it with me in real-time in front of the world. I don't know why I want to protect you, just that I want to."

I kissed her forehead, "I am sorry, my love. I am so sorry

because I love you so much and want to stop it, but know I am there with you. You can always call me—"

"I know. I know, Cal."

She handed me the envelope with the ultrasound pictures. "For now, the best thing you can do is take this home. Put it on the fridge. And don't argue with me."

While I always hated to put anything on the fridge, I agreed. "Sure. It definitely has a place on our fridge."

Daphne smiled, then looked down at her phone, immediately going back to gloomy.

"What?" I asked.

"The wedding planner," Daphne sighed. "So many questions. I just can't handle that right now."

"Let me handle it," I said.

"You can't. It's about my wedding dress," Daphne said. "I need one. I don't want to look at anything because all they're able to pull is ridiculous pregnancy-friendly dresses and I don't want that."

I tucked a curly strand behind her ear. "Daph, we'll figure it out. Just tell her you don't have the bandwidth and to bother me while you're away."

"Cal, that's—"

I kissed her, stopping the downward spiral. "Shhh. I will handle it, baby. Let me just appreciate one last glance of you—a happy you. I don't want to ruminate on things that bother you right now, Daphne. I don't have any time left for that."

She brushed my cheek. "I love you for that. I will have them bother you, then. I am officially stepping away."

7. DEMONS

Daphne

I STEPPED INTO A COURTROOM, SHAKING LIKE A LEAF NEXT TO MY sisters Delanie, Dora, my mother, and Chloe. Chloe insisted that if Cal wasn't coming, she was. Somehow, in this process, she'd stepped into the role of another sister. And since my pregnancy got outed, she'd only felt stronger. I sensed that I was the sister she never had. Either way, having more women on my side comforted me. I had an army of smart women behind me.

Delanie held my hand and whispered, "It's just a courtroom. You know what to do."

I shook my head as we took our seats behind the prosecution. "I haven't."

"But you're… a lawyer."

"I didn't practice criminal law."

"Not even in an internship?"

I looked up and saw the man of the hour entering the room in a tailored suit next to his expensive defense attorney. His hair was freshly cut. It was like nothing happened to him. Somehow, even the threat of prison couldn't bring him down. I shivered.

"The person I interned with is currently on trial. The man

has never spent a day in criminal court until now, either," I whispered back.

Chandler turned around, but missed our side of the court. Instead, he smiled at his parents.

"Where is the other woman?" Chloe asked.

"She's on bed rest," I whispered. "If you believe the *Mail*. Overdue."

"Shit," Chloe whispered.

"Leave her alone," I said. "She's a victim, too. Just like me, he groomed her. And now, he saddled her with a baby."

"And he's about to lose everything," Mum added. "Poor thing is in for a reality check."

I hoped they were right. I hoped that Chandler rotted. I also felt genuine pain at the thought of a young woman being forced to raise a baby alone knowing that the man who impregnated her—the one who promised her everything—had done something so unforgivable. He'd lose everything. I hoped at least she'd get to live off our divorce settlement for a minute.

We sat through opening statements. I wanted to vomit—both from the pregnancy and the nerves. And the longer I sat, the more I had to pee. But, I *couldn't* pee. Because I was stuck here. There was then a discussion of evidence and the long-awaited tape—the one the jurors swore they'd never seen—played.

The jury was a surprise to me. Though common in the US for low-level offenses, they were rare in the UK for anything less than a very serious crime. It hammered home the importance of the case. I didn't watch the video. I stared at the jury, taking in their appalled reactions to the video. I couldn't tell if it was me— naked for all to see—or the way I looked strung out and coerced that bothered them. I dropped my eyes, feeling so sick, and fiddled in my purse for a piece of paper, finding an old receipt, and passed it up to the prosecutor.

* * *

I'm pregnant and I really need to wee. -DD

* * *

It was the best I could do and I couldn't be too proud. More than that, I needed a minute for quiet.

At an opportune moment following the horrendous video the prosecution requested a short recess at which point, one of his direct reports led me to the bathroom along with my Mum who refused to leave me behind.

Inside a cordoned off bathroom, I relieved my bladder but also had a bit of a cry sesh.

"Darling, it will be okay," Mum said. "But you will not let him own this. Did you see the faces of those jurors?"

I flushed the toilet and left the stall, proceeding the to sink. Speaking to her reflection on the mirror before me, I said, "Yes. And do you know what they thought of me?"

"That you didn't deserve this," Mum said. "That he forced you to do this and then leaked it to the press."

"I know," I said. "But…"

"There is no but,"

I turned off the taps and dried my hands on a paper towel.

"You're going to be okay," Mum promised. "You will answer their questions and hold your head high because you are my daughter. And they will nail his ass to the wall or they will have to deal with me."

Her voice was strong and her face gentle as she pulled me close and squeezed me tight. "You are so strong, Daphne. Your have your father's desire for righteousness and my stubbornness. You will be fine."

"I want you to be right," I sniffled.

"It *will* be right. Okay. You will be fine. You are too good for him. You always were. You have a family behind you—a lot of angry women—and Cal. We will take care of him. We will end things for him. He won't do this again, Daphne, because *you* spoke up."

I nodded, trying to be brave, and patted my stomach, centering myself. It was all I could do.

"You have built a good life, Daphne. A life on your own—"

"Yeah, but what if this is the moment that…" Tears welled and my throat tightened. "What if this is the moment that everyone sides with him and decides I'm just some sort of whore who should have known better? And now, I get to raise this baby in a media firestorm when I am nothing more than tabloid fodder. And Cal will never be able to run for a second term and—"

"We have too much more to do, Daphne," Mum said. "You have done great things. And Cal will continue to do the same. And she… she will only know how brave her mother was, alright? She will believe only that her mother was great and strong."

Her hand rested on my belly.

"Mum, I don't even know—"

"I just have a feeling. And in six pregnancies, I was never wrong about any of you," Mum said.

I ignored her oracle predictions, but was grateful for my mother's compassion in the darkest moment.

"Now, you are a Delphine and a Carlisle. Chin up. Stiff upper lip. You will manage, darling."

And with that and tears dried, we left.

Walking back to the courtroom, my pulse raced. I took the stand shortly after, terrified of what could happen. Chandler smirked in a way that made me want to slap him. I snapped. My stubborn, enraged, calculating side came out. I *would* win this. I sat up, chin straight, and stared right at him. The smirk faded. He knew I wasn't giving in.

"Ms. Delphine, it is alleged that the accused distributed pornographic material without your consent in August of the previous year. Is that true?" The prosecutor began.

"Yes," I answered, hands shaking less.

"And this was distributed without any of your knowledge?"

"That is correct."

"Can you confirm what your relationship is to the accused?"

"He is my ex-husband," I answered.

"And at the time this allegedly occurred, was the accused still your husband?"

Unfortunately, yes. I responded with a stern, "Yes. Our decree was signed but not yet approved by the judge. We legally were still married. However, we were both in committed relationships elsewhere."

The prosecutor nodded and stepped back to grab a screenshot of the tape.

"I apologize for how hard this is, but I must confirm it. This is you, is it not?"

He showed me a photo of my drunken, likely drugged face, looking up at Chandler like an actress in a bad amateur porn.

"It is me," I agreed. "However, that tape was taken probably a decade ago. I barely recognize that woman."

"Understood. We all do change. Ms. Delphine, when did you find out about this tape's circulation?"

"My divorce attorney called and warned me. It was shortly posted on various news sites and social media—usually slightly censored—but the whole tape made it to adult sites quickly. I had to issue takedown notices. It was awful."

"And how did that make you feel?"

"Objection!" Chandler's attorney said, rightfully so. "Relevance."

The prosecutor sighed, "Withdrawn. Ms. Delphine, can I ask why you believe the tape was circulated?"

"I can only speak to my own belief," I said in my best legal way. "But, Mr. Walker was upset about his divorce settlement amount. This is well-documented in the numerous messages he sent to my email and phone. I gave those records to you all. However, I cannot confirm if the other intent was just to embarrass me. However, my belief is that he did want to hurt me in retaliation."

"An act of revenge?"

I nodded. "That is what *I* believe. Either way, he did this without my consent. That I know for a fact."

"Thank you. No more questions, My Lord."

The defense attorney rose at his desk as Chandler looked on.

"Ms. Delphine, did you originally consent to the tape being taken?" He asked.

"I said he could take it at the time—or I must have. However, I realize I was under the influence which speaks to the fact that I was *unable* to consent to both the act performed and the filming of said act."

The attorney smiled, satisfied. "Well, we've all done a little bit of that while drunk, certainly. Didn't you go to university?"

"I attended Oxford. I can say to this day the only partner who has ever come onto me when I was so out of it was Mr. Walker."

The court room murmured and the judge called for order. Once they were settled things continued.

"So, your current partner has never asked for something similar? You do not send intimate messages to him?"

I set my jaw, mortified that I was being led down this road. Thankfully, I was prepared for this and much worse.

"My fiancé would never do that, no. We established firm boundaries with consent soon into the relationship—largely due to my past history. Mr. Walker pushed this line frequently over the course of our relationship."

"So, you've never sent a cheeky text or video?"

"Objection. Relevance? Is the witness on trial?" The prosecutor called out.

"I will answer it," I said.

"Ma'am, I know you're a barrister, but I will be the judge," the judge said with a chuckle.

"It speaks to their relationship, which is relevant," the defense said.

"I will allow it, then."

I took a deep breath. "I do sometimes send cheeky text via encrypted messenger—as most couples do. However, I do not send these sorts of messages, no. But if I did, that would be between my future husband and me."

"Why did you allow this to be recorded?"

"Because he pushed me into it. I told him to delete it later. He swore he did. Obviously, he did not."

"So, Mr. Walker agreed to delete the video?"

I nodded. "Yes. And showed me that he had. However, I would now believe he kept a copy somewhere else."

"Have you ever done this with any other partner?"

"Objection—"

"Sustained," the judge said. "Mr. Park, can you please stick to relevant details?"

The defense attorney didn't show his anger. He'd planted the seeds of me being a whore in the minds of the jury and that was the whole point—cruelty to discredit me. Chandler crossed his arms, knowing the same. I turned from him back to my mother and sisters. And Chloe—the woman shooting daggers into the back of Chandler's head. It gave me strength.

"Ms. Delphine, did you not engage in electioneering to harm my client after learning about the existence of the tape?"

"Electioneering?" I cocked my head to clarify.

"Did you fly to the UK to meet with a shadow cabinet minister who is currently Home Secretary?"

"I asked him what he knew about the matter," I said.

"And interfered in an election."

"Objection—"

"Relevance, yes, yes," the judge said. "Can you explain your point, Mr. Park?"

"It speaks to motivation."

"I'll allow it," the judge sighed, annoyed.

"I am a citizen of this country. I was born here. I was a voter—"

"And you voted in this election?"

"No," I answered. "I left the UK. But there was no malice—"

"Ms. Delphine, is your current partner a member of the Democratic National Committee in the United States?"

"Yes," I answered.

"And did he give the keynote address at their recent party conference?"

"Yes," I answered.

"And did you—alongside him—host a fundraiser for a presidential candidate in October of this year?"

"I did not," I answered. "My mother did. And my mother is also a dual citizen who was born here. What is your point? Are you alleging I helped the Labour Party, which lost in a landslide? Or that I helped the Conservatives who ultimately won?"

"I ask the questions, Mrs. Walker."

The name set me over the edge.

"It is Ms. Delphine. I reached out to an old friend and colleague after hearing concerning things about someone distributing my tape to members of the party. Lest you forget, I was actively involved in politics here—as a citizen and the wife of a prominent politician. But he was also a friend. It was not some great political plot. I was asking for help. Is that not allowed?"

I felt the eyes of the jury and looked back to see several members glaring at the attorney. It was then that I realized I had the upper hand. Or, rather, I realized Chandler and I both recognized it. In what was hopefully only another few days, we'd have reason to celebrate a small victory—one that would restore me in a way I needed.

8. DOING THE RIGHT THING

Daphne

WE LEFT BRUNCH, TAKING THE DAY AWAY FROM COURT. I WAS about to have a mental breakdown and decided to take a day off of work, too. Delanie was only too happy to take the party to a posh place in Chelsea. We passed a window of a beautiful bridal shop. The renowned British designers had glorious dresses in the windows—happy dresses for brides who could be chic and wear whatever they wanted. My heart first fluttered, then immediately sank.

Chloe, walking beside me, stopped. "That dress is beautiful."

She looked at the same one I had an eye on—a sophisticated strapless ivory gown. It wasn't overly bridal.

"It's a wedding dress," Lanie laughed. "You have plans, babe?"

"No, but Daphne does."

Everyone stopped and stared at me.

"C'mon, Daph, I know you want to try it on," Chloe said.

"Let's do it," Dora delighted, grabbing my hand and pulling me towards the door.

"Dora Elizabeth! Do you think that is really appropriate? What if the paps see us out here?" I asked.

"Yes, total scandal!" Lanie rolled her eyes. "Woman who is about to get married tries on wedding dresses—"

"While the man who dropped her sex tape is on trial," I added, hands on my hips.

"Yes, whatever. Fuck him. Come on," Chloe opened the door and stepped inside.

Mum surprised me with a shrug. "You could use a cheer-up, darling."

By the time I made it inside, Chloe was in a full-on conversation with one of the consultants, pointing to the dress in the window, then me.

"It's just beautiful. But let's pull some others," Chloe said.

"Are you the planner?" The consultant asked.

"Daphne is my sister-in-law—will be," Chloe said.

"And can we get your name?" The older consultant behind the desk asked.

"Daphne Carlisle-Delphine," Mum answered.

The older woman did a double-take, then turned back to the tablet in her hand, but then went back to pure professional customer service, "Are you looking for something more under-stated? Simple?"

"Chic," I answered. "Sophisticated. I had a big ballgown for my first wedding. I want nothing like that this time. I want to focus on feeling beautiful and marrying the man I love. That's all."

She demanded, "Can you pull Geneva, Pippa? I would add Adelaide and Louisa into the mix, too."

I assumed these were the names of the dresses they saw me fitting into. As much as I wanted to be excited and happy, I just couldn't be. I knew that if a dress fit today, it wouldn't fit in six months. In the consult room, champagne emerged—something I couldn't partake in. I listened to my mother explain her own wedding dress to one of the consultants while Pippa zipped me into the strapless dress I'd dreamt up. The crepe fabric wasn't fussy like the intricate lace I'd worn to marry chandler. It was sexy in a way I'd never get away with for a UK church wedding. I felt a little like a bridal badass.

As I stood on the pedestal in front of a bank of mirrors, I fought *happy* tears.

"It's lovely on you," Mum said. "But I don't think any of these dresses will work, ladies. She hasn't told you but... she is... well..."

Mum couldn't bring herself to state the obvious. The desire for self-preservation in polite society overruled all else. Here—especially when w were back in the UK—she was Lady Danna first.

"She's pregnant, Mum. You can say it," Lanie insisted. "And happy about it. It was a happy thing."

"A surprise, but yes," I confirmed.

"Congratulations! When are you due?" Pippa asked cheerfully.

"August," I answered.

"And they are getting married in June," Mum said. "So this... it will not fit by then. We should find something... more suitable, I think."

"That's fine," Pippa chirped, noting my sad expression. "We will find something we could alter appropriately."

I was pulled out of the dress I'd fallen for and thrown into three beautiful dresses that they could make work—dresses I felt were anything *but* sexy, edgy, or sophisticated. They were traditional, stuffy, and princess-y. They weren't me.

"That is gorgeous," Mum gasped as I stood there in a beautiful white silk ballgown with an empire waist, long lace sleeves, and a high collar.

"It's too much like her other dress. God, Mum!" Delanie protested.

She was right.

"No. It's fussy. She doesn't want fussy," Dora spoke up. "I don't love it."

"I don't, either," I admitted.

"But it's so *classic*, Daphne. You would look darling. And it would hide your stomach."

I didn't want to hide my stomach. Tears welled and I sputtered, "I don't want that. I never said I wanted to just lie and hide this. I'm not ashamed to be pregnant. I know you might be, but… I am not! I'm finally having a baby with a man I can trust. After years of heartache, I'll finally be a mother. I refuse to feel bad about that! And I don't like it. I don't care if you do. The dress is lovely—for someone else. And you had your chance to dress me ten years ago. This is *my* wedding day. I will wear what I want."

Chloe handed me a tissue. I dabbed my eyes as my mother fell silent.

"Should we try the crepe on again?" Pippa asked, too cheerfully.

"Yes," Chloe, Delanie, and Dora answered in unison.

So, I tried on the dream dress again. I loved the ruching, the way it hit all of my curves. I felt like a woman. I felt strong. This was *the* dress, but I couldn't help but cry, because it was pointless. I couldn't wear this dress. It would never fit by the time we finally said our vows. So, once more, I gave up on a dream. My timing was always shit.

* * *

Cal

Chloe's number appeared on my phone as I was finishing my third cup of coffee. Worried, someone had died, I answered the phone.

"Is everyone okay?" I asked.

"Yes. Jesus Christ! Everything is fine. Calm the fuck down, dude," Chloe said.

I relaxed. "Sorry. You just never call unless someone has died."

"Okay, fair. No, this is not a life emergency—well, it's not a dangerous thing. It's more… well, your future wife fell in love with a wedding dress today."

"Okay… and the problem?" I asked, confused. "Is this a fight between Daphne and Danna, because I do not have the bandwidth—"

"No. I mean, yes, Danna preferred another dress but Daphne laid into her—rightfully so. Nah. She found this dress, Cal, and it was *perfect* on her. She cried happy tears. It was the first smile I've seen on her face in ages."

"So tell her to buy it," I said. "I'm not sure—"

"She won't. It won't fit her in June. She's being a realist, brother. But everything that they could make fit in six months made her want to cry sad tears. Your girl wants to look *hot* not matronly and it's… fucking sad."

I rubbed my left temple. "So why are you calling me? I can't fix that. It's very sad, but I cannot fix it, Chloe."

"I don't know. But… I'm letting you know."

I didn't know what to do with that information.

"Look, if there was any way to change the wedding date… could you? Move it up? Weddings are about the bride and yours is *sad*, Cal. I want to see her be happy. She fucking deserves that. Sitting in that courtroom with her tells me just how much she went through. Is there any way you could do it?"

"Chloe, that's… I'm not a miracle worker. Trust me."

"Think about it. Try your mayoral magic."

"Mayoral magic?" I laughed. "I cannot get alderman to agree on hotdogs or Italian beef for a luncheon. You flatter me, sister."

"Get it done. I believe in you."

And with no goodbye, she was gone.

I turned back to the day's agenda and a speech at a sustainability event. I arrived and chatted with people but my mind was thousands of miles away across an ocean. Kristy pulled me aside, sensing something was up.

"Are you okay?" She laughed.

"Unsure," I answered. "Honestly, I am worried about Daphne. This trial has been so hard on her. And my sister called me this morning. Anyhow, it's silly and I should let it go, but I cannot."

"What's silly?"

"Daphne fell in love with a dress and Chloe said it's the only genuine smile she's seen in ages. I know what she means. Daphne has been so down. This trial is wearing on her."

"It would wear on anyone. Reliving that all? No thank you."

"Sure. But Chloe said she came out of it for a minute, only to turtle back inward. And that's all I've seen. She beats down her feelings. The wedding meant a lot to both of us, but now it feels like she is just going through the motions to say she did it."

"So don't get married. Cal, you don't have to—"

"No. I'm not explaining this well. We both want this. She just would like to do it not seven months pregnant. And she'd like to do it in the dress of her choice. Chloe says she can't buy it because it won't fit her."

"Then get married sooner,"Kristy said. "Does it even matter if you walk away married? This is why marriage is silly to me. It's about the wedding—"

I rolled my eyes, "Kristy, I know it doesn't matter to you. It really doesn't matter to me, but it matters to Daphne. Her mother steamrolled over everything she wanted and she was basically forced to marry a man who betrayed her to save face. She makes herself so small."

"I remember," Kristy admitted. "But I am serious. Get married sooner."

"That is a logistical impossibility. You sound like Chloe! She thinks I have mayoral magic."

Kristy laughed until she snorted. "That's fucking great. Oh, I miss Chloe's wit in my life. She's right, though."

"Getting a venue, a caterer, a DJ or a band, everything?"

"Didn't you all just plan a huge engagement party at the Cultural Center? I got the invite by the way—"

"Yes, I saw you on the RSVP yes list," I said.

She furrowed her brow.

"What, I cannot look into who did and didn't RSVP?"

"I am surprised that you care, but okay. Who are you?"

"I am taking care of wedding planning stuff for Daphne. I don't want her focused on that right now with the trial."

"That's genuinely adorable. You're going to make a really good husband. Okay, well follow me here. The Cultural Center is a huge venue. A beautiful venue. I am assuming you already have catering, a DJ, bartenders, and all the complicated bits. It's a heavy lift, but you should enlist your mother and you can get it done."

"That sounds like a nightmare," I said. "She's been—"

"You need help. Everyone will be there. Just do the wedding and surprise your guests—and maybe the bride. If you truly want to take it off her shoulders, make it wonderful. She will be so relieved to just show up. I know I would be."

"And if I fuck it all up?"

"Enlist her female family members. Call your planner. Round the troops up. It will work. Be happy. Love that woman. And get her that damn dress."

It was a crazy idea, but I was left with only the wildest hairs to pursue.

9. DIDN'T DESERVE IT

Daphne

I HELD MY MOTHER'S HAND IN ONE HAND AND DORA'S IN THE other as I sat in a courtroom, back straight as I'd always been taught. I used my outfit to convey strength. I showed up in a dark teal dress—a color Chandler loathed on me and my favorite earrings. I wanted him to see me living proudly. The verdict awaited. It was either very good or very bad. Deliberations took only two hours—almost unheard of—and now we received the fated decision from the mouths of the people who held all my hopes—and Chandler's fate—in their hot little hands.

To my surprise, Chandler was relatively calm. He looked convinced this was all a good sign. After all, we both knew a quick verdict could be very good for a defendant. I hoped it was the opposite, that we won.

"We find the defendant—"

Dora squeezed my hand hardest. I knew her little heart was beating out of her compassionate little chest.

"Guilty."

I'd warned everyone *not* to celebrate this win, but Chloe still let out a little squeal of sheer joy on my behalf. Her squeal was largely unheard over the wailing of Chandler's mother and his very pregnant girlfriend who showed up to court.

The judge called us to order once more, and followed next steps while the women continued crying.

"When do they sentence him?" Delanie whispered.

"They don't. Not today. I have to come back for a victim impact statement in a few weeks," I whispered.

"What? Why?"

"It's just that way," I said. "It's like that in the US, too—except on TV."

Upon adjournment, I sat in disbelief watching a man I'd spent more than a decade with—a man I'd once loved with all my heart—be put in handcuffs and led away. His time with an ankle bracelet was over. For now, he would be in prison. Suddenly, he looked so small. The bailiff let him stand as his family and girlfriend hugged him tightly, the women sobbing as they did. It was surreal. He was gone. And likely, he was gone for years.

"Daphne, we should go," Mum said.

"I... I need a minute," I insisted. I just needed to see him led out to believe it.

"But darling—"

Her worries became clear as Chandler's mother barged up.

"I hope you rot in hell, you conniving little whore!" She shouted at me. "This was all because of you and your meddling—"

"No. You do *not* get to speak to her like that," Mum insisted. "You are embarrassing yourself."

"She had an axe to grind. She is so satisfied!" Chandler's mother pointed her finger at me, almost hitting Mum in the process.

"Excuse me, but do I need to throw hands or are you going to shut the fuck up?" Chloe clapped back, ignoring *all* social decorum. Her righteous indignation was what gave Elise Markham fits and made Cal proud.

"Is there an issue?" The Crown prosecutor stepped forward, his wig still atop his head. "Or will you please step aside, ma'am."

"I am allowed to have opinions!" She sobbed. "My son isn't guilty! He did nothing wrong! This is all this mob mentality. She called him a rapist! He is no such thing."

"He wasn't tried for rape, so I did no such thing," I insisted, annoyed.

"But he was," Chloe said. "And I will say that with my full chest."

"That is libel!"

"It's slander," I corrected her. "And if it's true, it's not defamation."

Frustrated with my legal clap back, she threw a small sachet of tissues at her husband and stormed out. Following close behind was Natasha, the woman he'd left in the lurch. Her parents were prominent Tories but were nowhere to be found. As the party deserted Chandler, I worried they deserted this girl, too. She wasn't even twenty-five. She was a baby. And now she was *having* a baby.

"I... I do not know what to say," she said, stopping.

"Then move along!" Delanie barked.

Natasha appeared remorseful, so I spoke up. "It's fine, Lanie."

"I'm... I don't mean to cause trouble," Natasha said. "What we did was wrong. And what he did... was unforgivable. I do love him, but... what he did hurt you. I am sorry."

Without thinking, I took her hand, tears welling. In the most maternal way, I said, "You, too, were a victim, Natasha. He did the same thing to me. I hope someday you can find peace with your child. She didn't do this. He did."

"But it was me—"

I cut her off. "It was you that woke me up, honestly. You gave me the strength to leave him. Please do not think that I blame you, sweetheart. That isn't it."

Tears ran down her face. She gave a small, weak smile and nodded. "You are kinder than you should be. I am dreadfully sorry. At the very least, just know that it will pain me to know how I enabled him. And I will sit with that. All I wanted to do was make a difference and—"

"You were sucked in. I get it. I was there. He was my boss once. Natasha, you are so young. Please, go on with your life. Do something for women and we will call it even," I said. "And if you haven't hired a family law attorney, please do. Do you know the name of my barrister?"

She nodded. "God, do I ever!"

"Ring her when you get home. Tell you that I sent you."

She cocked her head.

"You need her. She will gladly take you on."

Natasha nodded again. "Thank you. I don't deserve this."

As she departed Mum stared at me, mouth agape.

"What?" I asked. "She's a child. I won't curse her. What she did hurt me, but I won't blame her for his sins. I hope she leaves."

"Leaves and gets her bag," Chloe snickered.

"It was the greatest act of parental kindness I have seen from you," Mum agreed. "Daddy would be so proud of your compassion and strength, Daphne. Now, I am desperate for supper. Can we please take ourselves somewhere with food?"

I replied, "I suppose I could eat, too."

* * *

Cal

I woke to rustling in the corner of the room. I spied Daphne disrobing and throwing her clothes in the hamper.

"Is it done-done?" I whispered as she darted around the closet in near-darkness.

"I tried not to wake you," Daphne said, coming back to bed in one of my t-shirts.

70

"You don't have to worry about that. I'm glad to have you back."

Daphne settled into my arms, reseting her head on my chest and let out a long, happy sigh.

"I love you," she said. "I missed you. And yes, it is done-done."

Daphne had gotten on a plane late after the sentencing hearing, flying back private. By the time the verdict was released, I was knee-deep in an alderman meltdown, followed by a fundraiser. By the time I made it home, I went straight to bed.

"You didn't hear?" Daphne asked.

"I didn't check. I wanted it to come from you, Daph."

"Well, he got walloped—for this charge. Two years in prison and the maximum fine."

"Two years? That's a joke!"

She looked up at me, "That is the maximum penalty. Judging by the way his attorneys acted, they thought he'd walk away with nothing more than home monitoring."

"Shit. I'm sorry, baby." I kissed the top of her head. "For what he did—"

"He deserved worse, but he has no career left. He's isolated—"

"And he can live on his divorce settlement."

"That's unsure. His girlfriend wasn't there. I mean, she'd just had a baby, but if you believe the rumor mill, Chandler is about to be taken to court for support."

"Well, he's not making money in prison."

"Doesn't matter. He has assets," I insisted. "His assets will be enough to support them, I hope. I feel for that girl."

I held Daphne tight, taking in the smell of her. I was so glad to have her back.

"It feels like home with you here," I said. "I am glad this is over for a million reasons, but most of all because you're home for good."

"I was barely gone—"

"Daph, any time I am apart from you is too much."

"You sound like a sap," Daphne giggled.

"I am. For you I always will be. How are you feeling?"

"Today, better," Daphne said. "This past week has been better. I'm a little spooked, but I guess we will see what happens at the ultrasound appointment. We still haven't gotten our results back, of course."

"I meant about the whole thing," I said. "The trial and life now?"

She sighed long. "I... I guess I'm okay? This is the next chapter—a new step. I told myself this would bring me peace, but... I don't know. With so much changing, I feel like I'm leaving a part of myself behind but I don't know the woman before me."

"Daphne, the woman before you gets to live her life without constraints."

"I just... I want to get our lives on the road. I want to marry you and live. I want to know this baby will be okay and start our lives together. I want to put the past behind me and own my future."

"And you will," I promised.

"Then why do I feel like I am stuck in this grey area?"

I kissed the top of her head. "You've been through something unimaginable, baby. You were tested and pulled back into the abuse—and very publicly so! I think it is okay to feel a little out of it. Give yourself time. Just enjoy the quiet now."

She paused, then said, "You're right. I need to give myself more credit. This was exhausting. And being pregnant alone is a lot. I love you, Cal. I love you so much."

"I love you, too. And you will feel better after this appointment."

"I hope so," Daphne said. "I hope we will get some good news."

"We will," I said.

"I missed you so much," Daphne said. "Just this... the safety and the quiet. I could just go on like this. Thank you."

"For what, baby?"

"For just… being good. For just being honest and here for me. This year has been a disaster. We haven't even made it to the anniversary of Dad's death. Cal, it hasn't even been a year, but it feels like a good forever all the same."

"A good forever?" I asked.

"Because I feel like you were always meant to end up with me —and me with you. But it doesn't feel like an eternity in a bad way."

I kissed her slowly, understanding what she meant. It took us time to get here, but now that we were, I couldn't imagine life without her. It wasn't fleeting. It wasn't scary.

I pulled back and said, "There is nothing missing."

"What?"

"There's no sense of some big elephant in the room," I insisted, tucking her hair behind her ear. "You are the most wonderful person and I feel completely and utterly sure of this."

"Well, then, I guess you should marry me," Daphne snickered.

"I cannot explain it, but… I have always had a 'what if' playing in the background. With Kristy, I knew she couldn't give me what I wanted—even if I refused to admit it. It wasn't that I wasn't committed. I just wanted different things. With you, I was always hook, line, and sinker, Daph."

"It just took us time to be on the same trajectory," Daphne agreed. "I must admit I kicked myself many times for listening to you in that elevator. I think about the what-ifs of it. What if I'd been brave enough to send Chandler home and love you anyway? What if I'd just called you out—"

"I wasn't ready," I admitted. "I wasn't going to settle down or risk my career then. I was stupid to think you weren't worth it. I'm ashamed of it, Daphne. I think about it, too. But the truth? I wasn't mature enough to love you like you deserved—to put you first always."

"Why now then?"

"I have watched everything slip away. I knew what I wanted.

And what I wanted was this—a peaceful life with someone who is there at night. A life where I am free to dote on you, but where you do not need me to always rescue you."

"I can save myself. You remind me of that enough."

"And you do." I smiled down at her. "You are beyond wonderful, Daphne. I am so lucky."

"You're also nuts."

"A little. But who isn't?"

She ran her index finger down my chest and bit her lip, knowing it would send me over the edge. Suddenly, I was awake and wanting much more than to roll over and go to sleep.

"You want to fuck me, don't you?" Daphne asked.

"Yeah if it's not too much to ask. Only if—"

She cut me off with a long, hungry kiss and pulled my hand down to her center.

"You think you can be demanding, princess?" I asked, pressing her back against the bed.

"Am I not allowed, Cal?"

"Oh, no, you're allowed. Always. What do you want, princess? I want to hear you say it."

"I want you to unravel me," she commanded. "And to watch me cum. I want you to watch what you do to me."

Delighted, I tossed her panties aside.

"I want to listen to you cum. I want to watch what I do to you, yes, princess," I growled. "But first, I want to taste you."

"I…" Her eyes grew wide. "I…"

"You will say yes, Daphne, because you'll never deny me this, will you? The sound, sight, and taste of you, princess."

She bit her lip and threw her head back as I played with her clit.

"Sit on my face."

"Cal—"

"No. No excuses," I said. "Sit on my face, Daphne."

She gave me a combative look—mostly for show—before she fought a smile and followed orders. I reminded myself it had been *ages* since she rode me face like this. And yet? I loved lapping her up and listening to her panting, losing herself, earth shattering climax. I lived for the ways her legs quaked around me.

"I don't… it doesn't. I won't—" She protested, but stopped, breath becoming frantic.

No cumming during oral? I fought a snicker since that *never* went down. Daphne would cum—and hard.

"Oh, fuck," Daphne moaned. "I've been… so fucking… horny…"

Every gyration of her hips brought her closer. My grip on her ass tightened.

"Oh, fuck! I'm going to… lose.. it," she panted, gripping the headboard. "Cal, oh fuck! Oh! God!"

She came as loudly as I could remember in recent memory—whether for my benefit or due to being so desperate—and I got to taste her properly. As her legs twitched and she panted, coming down from her high, I gave her a spanking.

"Give me… a sec," she said, breath even more ragged. "That was… the world's longest… orgasm."

She fell to the side, flushed and frayed at the seams.

"You're complaining about a long orgasm, princess?"

Daphne shook her head. "No. I just feel like it took forever to come down. It was so good."

She curled around me. Instinctively, I kissed her forehead.

"Cal," she said quietly.

"Yes, baby?"

"I'm sleepy."

I snickered. "That's okay. We'll pick it up another day."

I'd get the best of her another time. For now, I had enough material for this week's spank bank and then some.

PART III

THE MERGER

10.A SLIGHT ISSUE

Daphne

"Fuck, Daph, slow down."

I was a woman crazed. After falling asleep yet again before Cal could get to bed, I felt I owed him *something*. He took care of me nonstop. Why wouldn't I do the same for him?

I looked at him from where I knelt. "You don't want this?"

"Oh, God, I do. But damn it, woman, all I did was make you tea!"

If he didn't get up at the asscrack, I could have woken him up like this, but the idea of going down on him in the kitchen still pleased me to no end. It was dirty, unexpected, and good all at the same time.

With no further protest, I went to work, taking his head in my mouth while I worked his shaft with my right hand. I bobbed slowly, focusing my efforts on the tip of his cock as I worked.

"Fuuuuuck," he groaned. "Daph, all I want... oh God."

"What?" I murmured using my tongue to lick the head of his cock.

"I just... fuck... I don't deserve you is all."

But he did. So, I ignored his half-hearted protests, taking him in—this time deeper. He dug his hands deep into my hair as I bobbed, enveloping Cal's cock with my mouth. I only did this for him. He was the only one I trusted not to force me or take advantage of my willingness.

"God, I love you," Cal moaned. "You are... so fucking good. Oh, fuck!"

He was so close. I ignored the sound of both our phones vibrating on the marble kitchen island to my left. Messages could fucking wait.

"I'm gonna cum, if—"

I didn't stop. I wanted him to. He always tried to warn me. It was another way he took care of me. It only made me love him more. I took deep and swallowed as he came hard, gripping my hair for dear life.

"God damn, Daph," Cal panted as I pulled back. "Jesus, woman!"

I wiped my mouth with my hand.

Cal pulled my chin up towards him. "You're so gorgeous woman. And when you take it so good? I can't help myself."

"I know," I stood back up, returning to my tea.

"What got into you?"

"I've been so horny and you've been so good to me. I wanted to return the favor."

"I know that's probably complicated, so full disclosure I'd never ask—"

"It actually doesn't worry me, Cal," I said. "You are so safe. It's one thing I've taken solace in this entire time. I never thought I'd ever feel so comfortable with anyone. I love you Cal. That is the honest-to-God truth. I swore I'd never remarry, but... you made the decision so easy."

He kissed me slowly. "I didn't think it'd ever happen for me, Daph, but I couldn't imagine it any other way."

It couldn't hold back. I loved this man to the ends of the earth and back. I brushed his face. "Thank you for loving me—loving us—like this."

He rubbed my stomach. "It's what you deserve, Daphne—

both of you." After a long forehead kiss that melted me once more, he turned to his phone. "Uh, Daph, the results are back."

That was the vibration I'd heard earlier.

"Should we read them?" I asked.

"If they didn't call us to say anything negative, that's good, right?"

"We can either wait for the meeting or—"

"I can't wait, Daph."

I beamed. "Then, let's open them."

I knew if they sent the results, we'd be alright. That was made clear by our OB. This was the moment we'd find out about the sex of our baby. To me, it didn't matter, but I *was* curious if Mum's spidey-senses checked out again.

"I love you, Daphne," Cal said, opening the email. "Nothing changes here."

"I know," I said, watching him scroll.

"No elevated risk, no elevated risk," he repeated aloud, as if needing a verbal confirmation. He reached the end, just above the sex and said. "I can't read it."

"Baby, the worst part is over,"I laughed.

"Well, I… you read it."

I obliged, smiling as it confirmed what Mum thought.

"Well, Mum was right. We're having a girl."

And with that, Cal swept me up in a big kiss. "I'm so excited, Daph!"

I laughed, taking his face in my hands. "I am, too."

"She's going to be spoiled within an inch of her life—by all of us."

"I cannot wait," I admitted. "It's perfect somehow."

Somehow, everything felt bigger and brighter. This baby was really happening. I was going to *finally* be a mother—with the person I trusted most. I'd chosen well. The timing mattered less than ever. This was meant to be.

* * *

Cal

"Cal, hello!"

I looked up as Judge Mahony appeared in the doorway. "Your assistant said—"

I stood, holding out my hand. "Thanks for coming by, John."

"It's been too long. I had you on my docket. They said your date changed—"

"I knew we invited you to the party tomorrow," I said. "But you are the officiant. So… can you officiate?"

"Of course. Your date was always held—"

I shook my head. "No. Tomorrow night. I decided to surprise Daphne tonight. She's expecting and… doesn't want to be big-as-a-house pregnant when we do this."

He did a double-take. "That is a… bold move. Are you sure—"

"Her family has been helping me. They even helped with the dress. It was the whole reason I started thinking about it. And my sister—"

"She really doesn't know?" John asked.

"No. I was going to surprise her—"

"Cal, you need a marriage license for me to officiate. This is… unconventional… but seems on-brand for the whole Delphine family."

I snickered. "Yes, David could be *impulsive*. But this isn't Daphne. It's me. She makes me a little crazy."

"First of all, congratulations on the baby. I should have said that first. That's such a happy thing."

I smiled. "We're both very excited even if the timing isn't super ideal. But, we already had the venue. She wants to wear this dress and not be miserably pregnant. I am trying to make it work—"

"That brings me to point number two. You need to get yourself to the County Building and get the marriage license today. It is good tomorrow, but I cannot marry you without it."

"Oh." Panic set in. "Really?"

"Yes. Quickly. Because it could take a few hours."

"I didn't think about that detail," I admitted.

"I think they might give you special treatment, buddy." John chuckled. "I'll call ahead and tell them the mayor is heading over."

I blushed. "I feel like an idiot, John."

"Nah. You're just a man trying to keep his soon-to-be-wife happy."

"She's gonna probably kill me."

"Yeah, no. She won't. She might give you a little grief, but I think she wants this or you wouldn't have attempted the stunt, right?"

"Probably not. Thanks, man. I appreciate it."

"Now, I will get myself together for tomorrow. I need details on your planned script, though. Just shoot me a text later."

"We want to do our own vows," I said.

"You were surprising her and planning on that?"

I winced.

"I'm glad you called me in," John chuckled. "Go get her and get this all wrapped up, man."

As he left, I looked at Daphne's calendar. We had a three-hour window to get this done by some miracle if I raced there like my legs were on fire. I emerged. "Sandy, hold all my calls. I need to go to the county building. And... I need you to reschedule my one if I'm not back."

She furrowed her brow.

"Daphne and I are getting married tomorrow—don't say anything. That was why the hold was on my calendar. I need to get a marriage license."

She erupted in a smile. "Well, don't wait around. I will transfer them to the deputy mayors as-needed."

"Bless you," I said, rushing out on a mission.

11. COVERT OPS

Daphne

"Cal?" I murmured to myself, standing in the hallway. I was just leaving the conference room with Chloe and our CMO when I spied him talking to my assistant.

"What the hell is he doing here?" Chloe laughed.

Cal heard Chloe first, but his eyes met mine and he was on a mission. He raced over, looking like the world was ending. My heart sank.

"Cal, do not say our party is cancelled," I said, sensing it had to do with tomorrow's evening plans. "I took the day off—"

"No, no," Cal shook his head. "I need to speak with you in private."

"Oh… okay," I said.

"Hello to you, too," Chloe said.

"Sorry, Chlo. Later. I just… I am in a rush," Cal said. "It has to do with tomorrow plans."

"Oh," she said, as if in on a secret.

"Can you all go ahead without me?" I asked. "And tag me in later?"

"Gotcha," Chloe agreed. "Come on."

She and the CMO left.

"Do you like your current CMO more than your past one?" Cal chuckled.

"My past one was an impossibly good-at-everything asshole," I said, marching over to my office. "But damn he was handsome."

Cal, flattered, closed the door. "Daph, I need you to just… not kill me."

"Cal, I don't… what did you do?"

"I planned a surprise wedding. I was going to tell you tomorrow, but I just met with Judge Mahony and he reminded me that we needed to get a marriage license today if we were getting married tomorrow."

"What? Tomorrow?" I slumped on the couch. "Cal, what the fuck?"

"Sorry, baby. I… I love you?" He winced.

"That's not a question," I said. "Why?"

"We had the venue. We had the date. And you didn't want to be *that* bride, remember?"

I beamed. "You did all this for me?"

"I did. Because I wanted to make you happy."

I normally avoided any physical affection in the office, but not today. I pulled Cal towards me by the lapel of his suit jacket. It was the strangest grand gesture. It came out of nowhere. I usually hated surprises, but this was next-level.

He pulled back. "I want to do *a million* things to you, Daph, but we need to get to the County Building, now."

"Okay," I agreed. "Let's go."

We raced out, me leaving instructions for my assistant. The car made its way towards the county building. It wasn't a long trip, but I realized I didn't have any of my documents.

"Cal, I need my passport or birth certificate. And you do, too—"

"Shit! Change of plans!" He called ahead to his driver. "Detour. We need to go to the house first."

"Yes, sir," the driver called back, heading slightly north.

As I dug our passports out of the safe, Cal, fumbled in the room next door with something.

"Cal, what are you doing?" I called, annoyed.

Cal returned. "I wanted to show you something."

I turned to see him holding a white garment bag. My mouth dropped.

"Do *not* tell me that is a wedding dress."

"Well what else were you going to wear, baby?"

"I hadn't thought that through."

"Well, I did. Chloe called me from London demanding that I fix things so you could wear this dress. And… here we are."

"The dress? The one I fell in love with?"

Cal nodded.

I jumped up, kissed him, and then panicked slightly. "I love it, but… what if it doesn't fit?"

"Chloe had them send the next size up," Cal said. "We thought about that. And your mother has a seamstress on call after you try it on tonight."

"That is… insane. Wait, you included my entire family in this?"

"I did," Cal said. "And Mom? She's been boxed out. She'll be happy on the day, but… I didn't want her contributions. Your sisters, Chloe, and your mum have been so helpful. I love you, Daphne. I wanted so much to make you happy."

Happy tears welled. "This is *so* unlike you, Cal, but I am over the moon. Thank you for this. I am… blown away."

"Then just say you will, okay?"

"Anywhere, anytime," I promised. "Let's get the damn wedding license so we can go through with it."

* * *

Cal

I woke, sleeping in too late, but after a night of pre-wedding celebration, I couldn't help myself. Daphne looked like an angel sleeping. So, I got up to make us some warm beverages in the kitchen. My heart was full. Today, I would marry the woman who'd always been right for me. It wasn't the way either of us expected it, but when the timing was right, we made it work. And even if it wasn't—even when the baby showed up—it still was. By the fall, we'd be a family of three with a perfect little girl. A year ago, I didn't even expect to fall back into anything with anyone. I was mourning the loss of my best friend.

It hit me. The one person I most wished was here—the one who would have given a hell of a speech—wasn't here. David was gone. It would be a bittersweet day. I thought of Daphne's worries of walking the aisle and shot her brothers a text. After all, they were in on the surprise by now. They thought I was nuts.

ME

Hey, so Daphne knows now. We had to get a marriage license.

DAVEY

Did she kill you?

ME

No. She's happy.

DERRICK

You got lucky. She must love you, dude.

ME

I hope so.

I neglected one detail. Your Dad is gone. She's worried about walking down the aisle without him.

DAVEY

I'll take her. I assumed I would.

ME

I am not sure what her preference is. But… if she needs someone?

DAVEY

Of course. It would be an honor. She's my sister. And I'm not about to desert her on her wedding day. You didn't even have to ask.

DERRICK

We aren't mad anymore. I promise no one is going to punch you.

DAVEY

Other than your mother.

I snickered, he wasn't wrong.

ME

Touché, Davey. Pray for peace. She'll text you when she gets up.

DAVEY

Sounds good. Don't get cold feet.

ME

I never would.

I continued making breakfast and loading the dishwasher with plates from our impromptu fourth meal of pizza at midnight when Daphne emerged.

"I was going to do that," Daphne protested.

"No, princess, you're getting the day to *rest* before we party later," I insisted.

She gave me a quick kiss. "I love you."

"I love you, too."

"I need to work on my vows. Did you—"

"Oh, mine have been written for weeks," I snickered. "I'll leave you to it and go to the gym, if that's okay?"

I knew she'd want some space. She longed for a quiet moment this morning.

"Yeah. That would help me focus."

"Uh… actually, I have one more question."

"What?"

"You know how you worried about coming down the aisle. Davey is ready to escort you. He's expecting it."

She frowned. "I…. I love that he wants to do it, but… I decided I have another plan."

"I am sure he will be okay with whatever," I clarified. "As long as you are happy. He just knows this is hard for you. And he and Derrick promised not to punch me."

"I am glad we've made it past that," Daphne giggled.

"So what will it be?" I asked.

"Do you want to go down the aisle together?" Daphne asked. "Because… I'm feeling like that's what I want. I want to spend the day with you—not alone. We entered this together as adults —fully-formed adults who lived a life before falling back into bed together, right? And you're my partner in everything, Cal. It feels right."

I gave her a long kiss. "Whatever Miss Delphine wants, she gets."

12.SURPRISE NUPTIALS

Daphne

BEFORE MY FIRST WEDDING, I'D HELD ONTO MY FATHER'S ARM FOR dear life, afraid I was making the biggest mistake of my life. I told myself it was just nerves, but knew deep down it was wrong. And in the end, it had been. Today was different. Today, I wore a chic dress to match the grown up, empowered Daphne I'd become. I held the arm of a man I loved beyond reason. My favorite earrings and a bracelet I'd inherited from my grandmother tied me to the past as I stood out facing my happy future.

I still thought about what would have been if Cal and I ended up together that year—if I'd stayed in Chicago—but he was right, we couldn't change the past and the timing was off.

As we hid in a hallway, I looked Cal's way. It was perfect. I missed Dad. I wished he could be here, but I loved this man. It was right.

"You okay?" Cal asked. "You're not going to faint or—"

"No," I shook my head. "Cal, I love you. This is perfect. Dad would have been proud."

Cal smiled. "He would be so happy. I just wish he could be here."

"Same, but… in a way if he'd never asked you to watch over me and if I'd never found my way back to you, it never would have happened, right? He's here in spirit."

"He sort of ordained it," Cal snickered. "That's David."

"Making a deal—a merger—posthumously," I giggled.

"Sneaky bastard—in life as in death."

I rested my head on Cal's shoulder and said, "I don't want anything else. I couldn't."

Cal held my waist tighter. "Never."

"Cal?"

"Yes, baby?"

I looked back at him with all the love in the world. "I want the baby to be Delphine-Markham. I want her to have both names."

"That's probably good because I told John to announce us that way. We talked about it—"

"I know," I said. "But we should do it. I want the kids to have *both* names."

"Same," Cal said. "So, now we're talking *kids?*"

I blushed as the music picked up. "Is that terrible?"

"Daphne! Cal!" The wedding planner waved us over. Our guests were seated. It was time to go. There was no time for Cal to answer.

We took our places before slowly walking down the aisle. Any worries about my confession abated as I glanced at Cal. He was high on the feeling, not at all worried about my words. He loved me. Everything else faded. Our families and friends looked on. Dora Elizabeth, Dahila, Chloe, and even Elise Markham cried what I hoped were happy tears. Mum would never cry like this, but she smiled. These people wanted to be here for us. It was a perfect moment—more perfect than I ever dreamed up.

The judge began, "We gather today to join Cal and Daphne in matrimony today. Before I begin, the couple would like to welcome you all."

Cal and I looked out and I began other lose it. Tears welled. Delanie rushed forward on cue to hand me a tissue.

"Thanks," I whispered.

We turned back to one another, our gaze never dropping until Cal pulled out our vows—his written in his terrible scrawl, mine in my neat script. Hell, as bad as his handwriting was, I could only think about it with love now.

He elected to go first. "Daphne, I won't pontificate too long about my love for you, because I think it's pretty obvious, but I do love you. You are so wonderful—compassionate, loving, and supportive beyond measure. But what I admire about you most is your willingness to go to the mat for your family. And today, I am so lucky to officially be in that fortunate group."

I dabbed my tears that ran even more.

"You are so fierce, my love. And I know that you will be a dedicated partner and mother to our future children."

Children. Clearly, we were on the same page.

"And while that trajectory may have started *a bit* sooner than we intended originally, I wouldn't want to live this chaotic life with anyone else."

"Wait, are you pregnant?" One of my aunts asked.

I turned momentarily and nodded.

Those in the room who *didn't* know erupted, interrupting Cal's flow. He paused like the adept speaker he was.

"We're both really happy," Cal clarified. "But this wedding was rushed at *Daphne's* urging, not because of any external pressure."

I clarified, "I really just wanted to not be miserably pregnant."

I turned back to Cal, signaling he should continue, "I promise to show up, to take care of you, and to always be an equal player in life and parenthood. Daphne, you have made me the happiest man alive. And for that... I could not be more grateful."

"I couldn't either," I said, starting my vows. "Cal, I am glad I gave over to the love before me rather than ran from it. Things were messy. Things weren't always easy, but we never gave up.

And you? You taught me to accept love the way I never knew I could—and in a way I never know I deserved."

I sniffled, fighting sobbing tears. "Oh, God, sorry. I'm falling apart."

Cal squeezed my hands. "Take your time, Daph."

Delanie handed me another tissue and I took a deep breath. "You are so wonderful. You love me so purely and so fully. I have no doubt that you will always treat me with love and respect. I am so lucky, Cal, that it finally worked out. And I've never been so sure about anything in my life. I promise to always support you, love you, and trust you."

That last one brought tears to *his* eyes.

Delanie handed him a tissue and gave him a pat on the back, eliciting a deep chuckle from the crowd.

The judge waited for us to confirm he could move on with the rest. He picked back up with the ring exchange. Cal slid my wedding band on—with a little bit of force since my fingers were swollen. I did the same for him. And then, we were done.

"And with the power of the great state of Illinois, I pronounce you husband and wife."

Cal didn't wait a second longer to kiss me. And I could have swore that I held onto that kiss forever because I wanted to give our photographer the best view of a kiss, but it was mostly because I never wanted it to end. I wanted to bottle this moment —the moment when I finally became Cal Markham's wife and partner for life.

When we pulled back, Cal said, "I love you, Daph."

"You too, Cal. So much."

We turned to look at the crowd which was now on its feet cheering us on.

"And with that, I am so proud to introduce you to the Delphine-Markhams."

And we were. It was the best merger of my life.

* * *

Cal

"It was the best wedding I've been to in ages," Kristy said. "An ambush wedding where everyone was happy for the couple and no one seemed stressed."

I shook my head. "I was sweating bullets all day waiting for something to explode."

"You looked truly in the moment by the time we got to see you," Kristy promised.

I smiled. "I was. It was truly the best feeling."

She patted me on the back. "It was wonderful to see. You love her. She loves you. It was always the way it should have been."

"I always feel awkward admitting that," I said.

"Cal, we needed to find each other to find our partners. For me, that's what makes it even more beautiful. We both got what we needed in the end—our happily ever afters. And for that, I am so grateful. Thanks for inviting us."

"Your urging was what put this thing together. Thanks for being my gut check and friend, Kristy."

She smiled. "Anytime. Daphne deserves it. In a strange way, as happy as I am for *you*, I am even happier for her. She has so much light in her eyes. You've brought her back to the plucky girl who was never afraid to argue with you in a meeting."

I snickered. "You're right. But I'd like to think I just gave her some space to feel that way. It's all her. She's the brains."

I watched Daphne dance—totally caught up in the joy of the moment—with her sisters.

"Make her rest tomorrow," Kristy said. "She's going to be exhausted."

"I know. I don't even know how she's upright now."

"She's happy. She's love-drunk. It does wild things to you. Are you taking her anywhere for an *actual* honeymoon?"

"Well, since she's not going to be able to travel in June, I decided to bump that up. We're going to Hawaii in a few weeks."

Where it all began.

"She doesn't know," I added. "It's a surprise."

"You are *full* of them. I won't lie. I'm jealous. You would have *never*."

I snickered. "You hated surprises. They never worked out."

"So does Daphne."

"Daphne is… I know what buttons I can push. It's hard to explain."

"You're perfect together. I get it. You do not have to explain. Go on, pull that woman off the dance floor and make sure she drinks water."

I took Kristy's advice, finally getting Daphne alone for a minute. It was true that the newlyweds never got much time together at the wedding.

"We need to cut the cake," I said. "We keep putting it off."

She pulled me into a slow dance as the music changed, looping her arms around my neck. "Okay. I will cut the cake—and eat it—but then I want to go home."

I smiled. "That sounds lovely."

"I am so full," Daphne said. "I couldn't want more. I just want to grow old with you and do all the things."

I kissed her. "It's all both of us want—and need."

"Okay, let's tell them to do the cake. Do not smash it into my face."

"I would *never*," I gasped. "That's just dickish behavior."

"Just to be clear, that is a fireable offense."

"For certain," I agreed.

We flagged down the wedding planner who called everyone over for the cake cutting. It was the only traditional thing we'd done. Daphne was certain she didn't want to do a bouquet toss or a a garter toss—which she described as "cringe". While I agreed to both of those being ridiculous, Dora had protested the bouquet toss. She was *desperate* to catch that damn bouquet.

We cut the cake without even a minor smash and kissed quickly while people clapped. Everyone was so happy for us—even Mom who admitted it was a wonderful wedding and she was happy for us to be happy, too. She'd softened—taking my words in Daphne's office seriously. It was the wakeup call she'd needed.

"Now, I'm going to eat this cake!" Daphne declared. "And I want a second slice because these are tiny."

I hatched about piece out of the cake and handed it over. I kissed her once more and finally got her to sit down and take a minute. She scarfed down her two pieces of cake and finished mine off before I could. In the end, I wasn't much for cake, so it was fine.

"I love the strawberry filling," Daphne said. "You did well."

"I am glad it met your expectations."

"It was beyond. Well done, Mayor Markham. Another smash hit."

I leaned over, kissing her slowly.

"Oh, take me home already," she groaned. "I cannot handle it. I want to jump your bones."

It surprised me, but I would take it.

"We should say goodbye to everyone."

"If we do, then it will take forever."

She was right. "But isn't it rude—"

"We're the newlyweds. It's our own party. We can do whatever we want."

"Point taken."

We notified the planner, who called the car. And we got no further than Michigan Ave before Daphne kissed me—hot and heavy like I was the air she needed to breathe. I still didn't understand her impulsive side, but I loved it.

"Daph, we should wait," I chuckled.

"I don't want to," Daphne said, calling up to the driver. "Can we put the partition up? And just... drive in circles if we need to —take Lakeshore Drive. Hell, head to Wisconsin if you need to."

I chuckled. The driver got the drift and Daphne tossed my bowtie aside.

"Daph, where does this side of you come from? Where does

bad girl Daphne live? And why am I so lucky to see her this evening?"

"I love you. And I want every bit of you. Plus, I found out from Chloe that you're taking me to Hawaii and I'm a little horny just thinking about it."

"Fucking Chloe," I said. "Let's not talk about Chloe."

"Fair," Daphne said. "Just think about getting me off."

"Daphne—"

"That's not my name right now," Daphne growled, pulling her dress up. She guided my hand up her thigh until it was past the point of no return.

"Daphne, you aren't wearing any panties."

"As you know full well you love."

"God, I love you. Are you gonna cum for me, princess?" I played with her wet clit.

"Yes," Daphne gasped. "Don't fucking stop until you've gotten me off."

"Yes, ma'am."

And *that* was how I managed to get Daphne Delphine off in the back of a limo headed north on Lakeshore. It wasn't on my bingo card, but as she moaned my name and pulsed around my fingers, I didn't really want it any other way.

"Oh, fuck," she whimpered, coming back down. "We shouldn't have done that."

"And yet, we did," I said. "But I know you're going to want to do the same… and I want to wait until we get home."

"And then what?" Her nostrils flared.

"I'm going to fuck my wife on the new dining table she just ordered," I said. "Fuck her until she screams for mercy."

13.A GRAND ARRIVAL

Daphne

WE RETURNED FROM PARADISE SUNKISSED AND WELL-RESTED. I worried about coming back to 500 emails and Davey in a tizzy, but to my surprise, he took care of everything, sending me a message saying it was all good and to take the day to rest up. Instead of bothering with my email, we surprised everyone by attending Saturday dinner at my mother's.

As we arrived in the drawing room, Mum stood, dumbfounded.

"What are you doing here?" She gasped.

"We thought we'd come over," I said. "We got back this morning."

"You're so tan," Dahlia said, giving me a tight hug, then pulling back. "And really pregnant."

"Let me tell you, I was a little nervous wearing a bathing suit, but I got over it," I said. "It is what it is."

"Not a single person complained," Cal assured.

"And they wouldn't. Your tits are… fab. I'm jealous," Delanie giggled.

"Thank you?" I asked. "Why are you like this?"

"Because you know it's true."

"Well, sit," Mum said. "Cal, do you want a drink?"

"I'm good," Cal said.

To his credit, he hadn't really tied one on in ages. Cal wasn't much for getting particularly tipsy. When he was in public, he kept himself on a short leash like the good boy he usually was. But now that I couldn't drink at all, he was acutely aware he should not rub it in my face. I was desperate for a sip of whiskey from my mother's stocked bar cart, but I behaved myself.

We sat down across from Davey.

"I told you to relax," Davey said.

"And I did, brother. Promise. I appreciate you covering for me."

"I got used to it. Now, we are desperate to have you back, but it was a good tester for when you go on leave."

"Please tell me you're *actually* taking leave," Delanie said.

"Yes, of course," I said.

"She's taking three months. So she says," Davey said. "But I suspect she's going to try to come back."

"Are you taking any leave, Cal?" Mum asked.

"Oh, sure," Cal said. "I am sure a bunch of assholes will grumble about how I am not doing my job by parenting my child and supporting my wife, but… they can bitch all they want. I'm going to take a straight month, then we will see. I probably will go back part-time. We'll make it work, but I'm not giving up that precious time."

I beamed at him. This is why I loved him—even when it was politically dicey, he chose us. He always chose our family first. I never expected it, but always loved him for it.

"Good. Your father always made time."

"David cared," Cal said. "And he stood by his family."

"Well, if you have six kids, you better show up," Davey said. "That's not normal."

"It was perfect. You shush!" Mum chastised. "And you loved having siblings."

"Sometimes," Davey said.

"You always doted on the girls," I snickered. "You hush. Just you wait!"

"You'd have to find a woman willing to marry him, Daphne. Good luck!"

"Lanie!" Mum admonished. "Be nice."

"We're not planning on having six, for the record," I clarified. "Two is good. But we figure we will get this one here first."

"I cannot wait," Mum brimmed.

I looked at Cal, signaling I wanted to drop the big news. He nodded.

"What?" Delanie asked. "What now?"

"We wanted to say we found out what we're having," I said. "The sex of the baby."

"Oh yes?" Mum asked. "Oh good! You're not *those* people."

"It's okay not to say the sex of the baby, Mum," I groaned. "But no, I wanted to know. So we could give the baby a name. And I think we have one."

Cal smiled. "We do."

"We're naming the baby Cordelia Alma," I said. "After great-grandma and great-aunt Alma."

"A girl?" Delanie screeched, hopping up to nearly take me out with a hug. "Oh my God! Yes!"

"That's a lovely name," Mum said, fighting tears. "Two strong, independent woman for what will likely be a willful, opinionated child from the two of you."

Cal chuckled. "With her mother's stubbornness and my unwillingness to listen to reason, I bet you're right."

"It's for the best," Davey said. "I feel like you need a girl."

"Need one?" I snickered. "Why, Davey?"

"Because Dad always said you're not a real parent until you have to out-argue an articulate teenage girl."

Cal laughed. "Oh my God. What?"

"The girls boxed his ears in verbally—mostly *this* one!" She elbowed Delanie who rolled her eyes.

"God, I cannot help if your rules were always a joke!"

"It seems fitting. David loved them, though," Cal said. "Nah. I was raised by a strong, stubborn woman. I prefer women when it comes to accountability. They will always call me out on my bullshit—Daphne, Jo, Chloe, even Kristy. Sometimes I just need a smack upside the head."

"I prefer it, honestly," Davey admitted.

"This is why you will never find a woman. She shouldn't be your mother, David," Delanie said.

"Nah. Just someone willing to hold me accountable. Look, I'm not the brains of the family. I need a brainy woman."

"One will never choose you!"

"You two are in a mood," I giggled. "God. I missed this. It's been too chaotic."

"They are feeling competitive," Mum said. "We were discussing Cordelia's future prospects with a favorite aunt or uncle. Or, rather, they are getting competitive over something *so* ridiculous."

"There is space for everyone," I said. "She will be so blessed with people to dote she'll be spoiled rotten."

"Impossible," Cal said. "You cannot spoil a baby. I firmly believe that."

Mum rolled her eyes. "You and David. It drove me mad. Don't always make your wife play bad cop."

"Look, I cannot help if I've waited nearly fifty years to spoil a kid. I might be crazy, but the kid will be loved and have everything I didn't have."

I squeezed his knee. "And she will be so lucky to have all of this family."

"You must tell your mother," Mum said. "She will lose her mind."

"Oh, she *and* Chloe," Cal agreed. "Chloe was on Team Girl."

"I know," Lanie snickered. "She's already stockpiling clothes —even without knowing—and searching for ponies online."

"She's ridiculous," Davey said. "Keep this kid far from horses, Daph. Horse girls are the worst."

Delanie leaned across Mum to slap him. "You're an ass. Horses are good for kids. Every kid should have a pony. Even Cal agrees."

"No comment," Cal sighed. "But it's proof I love Daphne and Chloe to even entertain the idea."

I smiled. "If her aunt wants to buy her a pony, I will not stop her."

"That's just playing dirty," Davey said. "No one can top a pony. Derrick will have planes. I'm out of it."

"Just show up," Cal said. "She'll love you for it, Davey. We all will."

Cal squeezed my shoulders. I leaned my head on his shoulder, knowing it was the best part. He *wanted* them in our lives—even if it was messy sometimes. Even if there was sometimes drama and a lot of complication, even if there was Catholic guilt afoot. He wanted to be a part of our family and he wanted them to be a part of ours. It was perfect. It was what Chandler never would have given me and it was everything I wanted.

"Hello!" Dahlia's voice rang out.

"Drawing room!" Mum called back.

Dahlia came around the corner, her face erupting in a beaming smile.

"Oh my God, Daphne and Cal are here!"

She swooped in to hug us both. "Sorry I am late. I had to make sure nothing was going to fall apart before I left."

"It's okay," Mum agreed. "I told the cook we'd be late to dinner. Daphne, do you want to tell her the news?"

"Shit! Yes," I said. "Cal and I are having a girl named Cordelia Alma."

"Oh my God!" Dahlia said. "So perfect!"

It was. And as we took our places around the dinner table, Cal to my right, I couldn't help but brim with all the oxytocin in the world. *This* was my forever. This was what we always deserved—love, acceptance, and joy.

As we returned home, Cal made us some tea while I looked

out over the city from the living room window. It glittered. As we'd started that night in a conference room, it was the endless backdrop to *us*.

"Here you are, baby," Cal said, setting a mug down on the coffee table.

I turned, giving him a smile. Dropping to the couch, I stopped to appreciate the baby moving within me. The kicks had only just begun.

"She's moving?" Cal read my expression.

"Uh-huh."

"I'm still sad I cannot feel her," Cal said.

"Soon enough," I agreed, quietly sipping my tea. As the hot liquid hit my stomach, she picked up speed in protest.

"What are you thinking?" Cal asked.

"That I am forever grateful for this city. And I'm glad I stopped fighting my ties to it," I said. "That I just got over being a Delphine and stopped running from it."

He tucked a strand of hair between my ear. "You're always going to be a Delphine. And Cordelia will be, too."

"I know."

"You're David's daughter. There is no denying it, Daphne. You defend your family and legacy fiercely—with your whole heart. When you heard the call and when the time was right, you came home. And I am so glad it worked out."

I met his gaze. "When the timing was right and you believed in me. When I didn't, you did, Cal."

"Maybe, but it took your determination and persistence. Daphne, never doubt your own will to thrive. It makes me so proud. I am so happy to be your husband."

His words brought tears to my eyes.

"No, no, don't cry," he snickered. "God, I'm sorry."

"I just... I'd cry at a commercial right now," I said. "But it's beautiful. It all is."

"It's the best," Cal said. "It's our chaotic, beautiful happily-ever-after, Daphne."

EPILOGUE

Cal

I sorted through the nursery as Daphne called out, "It's chaos, but I am so tired. I cannot move!"

"It's fine," I said. "Go sit down on the damn couch, woman!"

I heard her mumble and waddle past the damn nursery. Daphne's problem wasn't a fear of giving birth. It was her stubborn approach to never slowing down. She'd been on leave since before her due date. She was now *overdue* and finally having contractions that looked like something. I basically had to force her to put on pants to go to the hospital. She was determined to stay here as long as she could—swearing it would never happen.

"The aquamarine one!" Daphne called.

"Yes, baby. I have it. I know which one!"

I finally pulled out the onesie she wanted—one Chloe had made custom with the Delphine's dolphin logo on it. Daphne waited until we were literally on the way out the door with a car waiting below to take us to the hospital to change her mind on the "going home" outfit. I didn't argue with the woman about to push a human out of her body.

"Got it!" I called back, shoving the tiny garment in the bag and packing it off to the door. When I reached her, she was standing by the elevator, staring down at her feet.

"Shit," Daphne said. "My water just broke. The car—"

"I will get a towel," I promised. "It's fine."

"We need to clean it up—"

"Just focus on yourself, baby," I said. "I will handle it."

I tossed the bag down on the ground by the elevator door and grabbed a slew of towels from the linen closet.

"Not the blue ones," Daphne cringed. "I literally just bought those."

"Daphne, this is *not* the time to worry about towels. I will buy you a dozen more if it bothers you. Hold this one."

She didn't protest as I raced away with the others, tossing them in the washer. She called the elevator. As we climbed on, I realized this was the last time we'd be here alone—a couple rather than a family of three.

"It's the end of an era," Daphne said.

"It really is."

She braced on the elevator railing, groaning.

"See, they are getting worse," I said, timing the contraction. "That was eight minutes, Daph."

She glared and straightened up, trying not to tell me that it hurt. I knew it did. She wasn't a baby about such things. By the time we made it to the hospital in horrible traffic, she finally let on how miserable she was. Making matters worse, we had a parade of press following us. As if this was the delivery of a royal baby, they'd be lying in wait outside for three weeks.

"I will walk inside, but get me a goddamn wheelchair. I feel like my body is falling apart, Cal."

"Yes, baby," I said.

It was only a few blocks, but it felt like a great expedition by the time we made it. And as we did, I assumed it would be a quick labor, and the baby would just come out. I couldn't have been more wrong, of course.

"Four centimeters," the nurse said. "We're making progress from your last appointment, though."

"I want an epidural *now*," Daphne insisted.

I looked at the nurse. "Sure. I will get the OB to put the order in."

Daphne got what she wanted. After some verbal abuse and a lot of swearing, Daphne rested quietly on the epidural. She napped, but I couldn't rest. I worried too much about everything that could go wrong. She'd been having contractions for twelve hours, but now they were ratcheting up. With the help of Pitocin, she moved along. It took around twenty hours total, but in the dark of night, Daphne was ready to push. There was no time to panic now. There was no turning back.

Once more, I didn't know what to expect. I thought, like in the movies, the baby would emerge after a few quick pushes. Instead, the reality was brutal. Daphne screamed, vomited, and sobbed with every push.

"When does it get better?" I panicked, asking a nurse as I placed another washcloth on Daphnes's brow.

"When the baby comes out," the nurse said, as if I were an idiot. "And she will."

"Cal, stop panicking. It's…" Daphne growled through another contraction. "It's not helpful."

"Okay, but this feels like a Hobbesian state of nature you're being put through."

"Cal, please don't go philosophical, for fuck's sake!" Daphne said. "I'm dying here."

"You're dying?"

"It's fine," the nurse holding Daphne's other leg said. "You're doing everything you need to do, Daphne."

I wanted to take her pain away. She was so miserable, even with the epidural. I expected it to cut all of the issues. Instead, she shook, sweated, and screamed.

"Daphne, on the next push, I want you to think about climbing a rope," the OB said.

"A rope?" Daphne panted. "Why?"

"It's just a visualization. Just climb it in your mind. Push with everything you have."

"It feels like my body is ripping in two!" Daphne sobbed.

"The epidural is wearing off, but the baby is *right here*," a nurse by the doctor's shoulder said.

"Daph, you are so strong."

"I don't know how Mummy did this six fucking times."

"You're tough—you all are," I assured. "And you can—"

I didn't finish. She bore down again, pushing against my hand harder than before.

"Motherfucking fuck!" Daphne screamed. "Fuck, fuck, fuck."

"Keep going! She's coming!" The doctor said.

And within a few seconds, The baby was there—in the doctor's hands first, then on Daphne's belly. Daphne went from screaming obscenities to sobbing happy tears. In fact, we both did. As Cordelia screamed at her distaste for life outside the womb, we fell in love with her. Relief washed over me. She was here. Life suddenly felt complete in a way I'd never imagined.

* * *

Daphne

I woke in the morning, hungry as could be. All I'd gotten was a deli sandwich the night before. It was a piss-take. I'd pushed out a baby—a whole eight pounds of human—to have a turkey sandwich and bag of chips. I wanted bacon and eggs desperately. Sitting up, I saw Cal sitting on the pullout sofa, cross-legged, just staring at Cordelia.

"You're up," I murmured.

He looked over. "Couldn't sleep. Too excited."

"I need you to sleep," I giggled. "Cuz this baby needs to be on a schedule."

"I'll sleep after breakfast. I hope you didn't mind that I put in the order—bacon, eggs, hash browns."

"Yes, please," I said. "Bless you. Did you feed her?"

"And changed her," Cal said. "I didn't want to wake you."

I sighed, looking down. "Yeah, well, it hasn't been a great success trying to feed her. I could try in a bit."

I was frustrated that my milk hadn't immediately come in. And since Cordelia was slightly jaundiced, they'd wanted to top her up with formula. I knew it wasn't the end of the world, but I wished things would have been perfect.

"Don't freak about that," Cal said. "It's going to be wonderful. Here, take her."

He deposited our daughter in my arms. She stared up at me, bright-eyed.

"I still need to pinch myself," I admitted. "How did this finally happen?"

"You deserved it. You worked really, really hard to get her here. So, of course, she's perfect. It's only fair."

I beamed at him. "She is perfection."

"She's a beauty like her Mom."

"With your annoying amount of energy."

He chuckled. "Let's hope that wears off, and she sleeps like her mother soon."

I kissed Cordelia on the forehead. She groaned and kicked her legs. Watching her fight the swaddle was my new favorite pastime. She hated it, but I knew it was good for her.

"Your mum wants to come today," Cal said.

"That's fine," I agreed. "She's welcome. I don't really want everyone here, though."

"I told Mom and the siblings they'd have to visit us later," Cal said. "But I figure since your mum is helping a bit, you wouldn't mind."

"I will oblige her. Why don't you go home and shower and nap while she's here?"

"Daph—"

"It's an order, baby," I said.

"Fine," Cal said. "But I don't really want to leave her."

"I know, but take the time to rest. Because once we go home, you need to be on baby patrol. I plan to do fuck all but nurse her."

"That was the plan. Fine."

Cordelia nudged me, rooting.

"Maybe she *is* hungry," I said. "Can you hand me a pillow?"

It was worth a shot. To my surprise, Cordelia latched. It hurt for the first few seconds, but I settled in as my first letdown kicked in. Relief set in. Maybe I would actually be able to nurse this baby. I'd only heard such things described with a "you'll know it when you feel it" comment.

"See, she knows what she's doing," Cal said. "Even if we are clueless. Instinct is crazy."

"You're doing a great job, Cal," I promised. "We will figure it out."

He leaned over and gave me a kiss.

"I'm just following your lead, Daph."

"Well, you're doing a great job. We're going to be okay. We'll muddle through the chaos—as ever."

"And fall in love all over again," Cal said. "Sorry, but… this is unexpectedly the best feeling in the world."

I smiled up at him as I cuddled Cordelia close. "It should be. It's the universe finally working out, Cal."

ACKNOWLEDGMENTS

Thank you to *all* my arc readers and readers obsessed over this couple. I hope that this made up for the parts you didn't get in *Executive Decision*. This book was life-changing in so many ways and I cannot wait to see how you react to this one!

LOVED IT?

Leave a review here or grab Davey's story, *Power Move*.

Want a preview of Davey's story? Click here.